"So, what brings you by, Nurse Reston?"

Rahman asked, his voice husky. "To see what a sheik looks like? To see how the mighty have fallen?" He choked on a mirthless laugh and reached for a glass of water.

Amanda automatically handed it to him.

He wrapped his fingers around hers, and Amanda felt a shock wave race up her arm. Despite the need to remain professional, she almost dropped the glass.

He was breathing hard.

So was she.

And, standing there locked in this endless, wordless gaze with him, Amanda knew deep down that Sheik Rahman Harun was unlike any other patient she'd ever had....

Dear Reader,

There's no better escape than a fun, heartwarming love story from Silhouette Romance. So this August, be sure to treat yourself to all six books in our sexy, sizzling collection guaranteed to keep you glued to your beach chair.

Dive right into our fantasy-filled A TALE OF THE SEA adventure with Melissa McClone's *In Deep Waters* (SR#1608). In the second installment in the series about lost royal siblings from a magical kingdom, Kayla Waterton searches for a sunken ship, and discovers real treasure in the form of dark, seductive, modern-day pirate Captain Ben Mendoza.

Speaking of dark and seductive, Carol Grace's *Falling for the Sheik* (SR#1607) features the mesmerizing but demanding Sheik Rahman Harun, who is nursed back to health with TLC from his beautiful American nurse, Amanda Reston. Another royal has a heart-wrenching choice to make in *The Princess Has Amnesia!* (SR#1606) by award-winning author Patricia Thayer. She survived a jet crash in the mountains, but when the amnesia-stricken princess remembers her true social standing, will she—can she—forget her handsome rescuer…?

Myrna Mackenzie's *Bought by the Billionaire* (SR#1610) is a Pygmalian story starring Ethan Bennington, who has only three weeks to transform commoner Maggie Todd into a lady. While Cole Sullivan, the hunky, all-American hero in Wendy Warren's *The Oldest Virgin in Oakdale* (SR#1609), is coerced into teaching shy Eleanor Lippert how to seduce any man—himself included.

Then laugh a hundred laughs with Carolyn Greene's *First You Kiss 100 Men…* (SR#1611), a hilarious and highly sensual read about a journalist assigned to kiss 100 men. But there's only one man she *wants* to kiss.…

Happy reading—and please keep in touch!

Mary-Theresa Hussey

Mary-Theresa Hussey
Senior Editor

Please address questions and book requests to:
Silhouette Reader Service
U.S.: 3010 Walden Ave., P.O. Box 1325, Buffalo, NY 14269
Canadian: P.O. Box 609, Fort Erie, Ont. L2A 5X3

Falling for the Sheik

CAROL GRACE

SILHOUETTE *Romance*®

Published by Silhouette Books

America's Publisher of Contemporary Romance

For Nancy Savage, international nurse, world traveler
and bonne vivante, with thanks for the help,
the years of friendship, and especially for
the laughs along the way. "Isn't life interesting?"

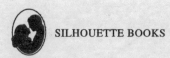 SILHOUETTE BOOKS

ISBN 0-373-19607-5

FALLING FOR THE SHEIK

Visit Silhouette at www.eHarlequin.com

Printed in U.S.A.

CAROL GRACE

has always been interested in travel and living abroad. She spent her junior year of college in France and toured the world working on the hospital ship *HOPE*. She and her husband spent the first year and a half of their marriage in Iran, where they both taught English. She has studied Arabic and Persian languages. Then, with their toddler daughter, they lived in Algeria for two years.

Carol says that writing is another way of making her life exciting. Her office is her mountaintop home, which overlooks the Pacific Ocean and which she shares with her inventor husband, their daughter, who just graduated college, and their teenage son.

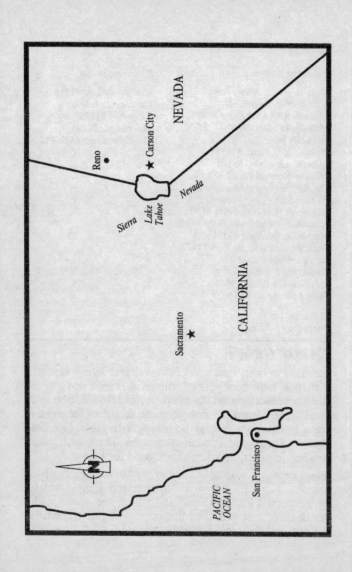

Prologue

Sheik Rahman Harun skied the way he did everything else—expertly, wholeheartedly and a little recklessly. It was the end of a perfect day at Squaw Valley and he was making one last run. Even though the sun was setting, he hated to call it quits. He loved the rush of the wind in his face as he was doing tight stem turns. It was getting cold, but he didn't stop. The snow, which had been slushy on the surface was now freezing into ice. He didn't want to quit. Not yet. Sure, he was tired and not as much in control as he'd been an hour ago, but he was following a giant slalom trail, his skis one inch apart, his boots touching, carving a single track through the snow. It was pure ecstasy.

It would have been even better if he'd had someone to share the fun with. Skiing with Lisa had been exciting. They'd had a friendly competition to see who could go higher, faster and take more chances. He couldn't quite believe she would never ski with him again. Even now, whenever he saw a woman in a bright red fitted ski jacket, her body curved gracefully as she sped down the hill, he felt the pain all over again when he realized it wasn't her. It couldn't be her. Lisa was dead.

Every time he got off the lift, he expected to see her with her goggles hanging around her neck as she reached out to grab his hand. One more run, she'd say. Come on, Rahman, just one more. But there would be no more. Lisa had taken her last run. He felt the tears sting his eyelids. He reminded himself that sheiks do not cry.

He stayed on the marked trails today. If Lisa were here she'd be leading him into deep powder in closed areas, taunting him to take a chance on getting lost or buried beneath an avalanche. When he'd try to talk her out of something risky, whether it was skiing or hang gliding or bungee jumping, she'd tell him he was no fun and she'd pout until he coaxed her out of it. One last challenge and she'd paid the price. So had he. They'd had good times, but those carefree days were over for good. Not only for Lisa, but for him, too. Nothing would ever be the same.

His twin brother Rafik would have loved the skiing today. He'd have been right there with him, every turn, every jump over every mogul. They'd learned to ski together as children on vacation in the Alps. They competed in everything—tennis, golf, racquetball and skiing. But Rahman was alone today. It was about time he got used to it. It was time to face the fact that relationships and friendships were all transitory. Nothing was permanent. Life was fragile and loneliness had a way of hitting him when he least expected it, like a sudden blast of cold wet snow.

Tomorrow a big group of his friends would arrive. That ought to help him out of his funk, but sometimes he felt even lonelier in a crowd. He missed Lisa's laughter. He kept thinking of the things they'd planned to do together. Take a safari in East Africa, take up snowboarding, bicycle through France. He could still do those things, but what was the point of doing them alone?

His brother wasn't available anymore, either. Rafik had recently gotten married which had left a big hole in his brother's life. Not that he didn't like his brother's wife. He did. But everything was different now that Rafik had someone to share his life.

With the sun gone behind the mountain the light had changed. There were no more shadows, no way to see the dips in the snow. The landscape became featureless and indistinct. His skis clattered when they hit the frozen snow. Then they skittered. He was going too fast and he was out of control. The ground rose up to meet him and he tumbled head over heels down...down...down. The wind whistled in his ears, the snow clung to his skin. His head felt like a rubber ball banging against an icy cement floor.

When he finally came to a halt, only a few feet from a snow-covered oak tree, every bone in his body felt shattered by the impact. He lay spread-eagled, facedown in a drift of snow, waiting for the pain to subside. Rahman wondered where his skis were. His new parabolic skis that allowed him to ski better than he'd ever skied before. The skis with the excellent bindings that released so he hadn't seriously hurt himself.

His mouth and his ears were full of snow and he ached all over, but he was okay. He was fine. Just a little sore and a little woozy. Fortunately his poles were still attached to his wrists. In a minute he'd get up and look for the skis then he'd ski down the hill and quit for the day. As soon as his head cleared and he caught his breath... He gave himself more than a minute. More than five minutes. Then he lifted his head, braced his arms against the ground and felt a spear of pain go through his chest.

Through a haze he realized he wasn't going to ski down the hill after all. He lifted his head and tried to yell for help, but the only sound that came from his lips was a moan.

Chapter One

The Northstar Home Health Agency of Pine Grove, California, looked more like a ski chalet with its peaked roof covered in snow and interior of knotty pine. It was as warm and cheerful as the owner and manager, Rosie Dixon, who beamed at her friend Amanda from behind her desk.

"Have I got a job for you!" Rosie said.

"Already? I haven't even unpacked my suitcase."

"I told you this is the land of opportunity. The golden state." Rosie spread her arms out wide. "Why else did you come?"

Why indeed? Why had Amanda quit her excellent job in Chicago and come running to this mountain community, two thousand miles away? There was only one reason. One big reason. Rosie didn't know and Amanda didn't plan on telling her. It was too embarrassing, too shameful, too awful.

"Because you finally came to your senses, that's why," Rosie said, always helpful, answering her own question. "I've been telling you to leave Chicago for years. I knew you'd love it here. It's paradise."

Love it? Paradise? Amanda looked out the window at the red-cheeked people walking down the main street wearing trendy wool caps, carrying skis over their shoulders and at the outline of the mountains in the background. Sure, she was used to snow in the winter, but not this altitude. She didn't ski, she didn't climb. Maybe she'd love it here, maybe she wouldn't. At this point it didn't matter, because she needed a change. She needed a change desperately. And Rosie had offered it to her.

We're short on nurses, physical therapists, you name it. We're short on all kinds of trained professionals. We've got plenty of waitresses and lift operators. College kids who are taking off for a year to ski, she'd said. But they're no help. Not to me. Not to the patients.

"What is it?" Amanda asked, slipping out of her winter jacket.

"What is what? Oh, the job, the job. It's a real challenge. Just what you said you wanted. A ski injury. Punctured lung, broken ankle, concussion, a few other complications. Still in the hospital, but champing at the bit to go home and recuperate. But home is in San Francisco so the alternative is to go to the family ski cabin. Doc says no, gotta stay in the hospital, patient says I'm outta here. I say if he agrees to the ski cabin I'll get him a private duty nurse. Not just any private duty nurse. Somebody with years of experience in trauma and intensive care. Somebody who's seen it all and done it all…" Rosie stood up and gestured dramatically. "My roommate and best friend from nursing school— Amanda Reston…ta da!"

Amanda admired her friend's exuberance. How long was it since she'd been that upbeat about anything? Rosie was right about one thing. Amanda had seen it all and done it all. That was why she was here. She couldn't do it anymore. Not there. Not with Dr. Benjamin Sandler in charge of her department. Either he had to leave or she did. She knew he wouldn't leave. Why should he? It obviously didn't bother him to see her every day at work the way it bothered her. And in her heart she knew it was time for her to move on. Then came Rosie's call. The same call she made every year, twice a year or more. But this time, more urgent, more insistent.

Come to California. See what it's like. Give it a chance. You need a change. And we need you.

So she was here. Reunited with her old friend and roommate. Despite marriage and twins, Rosie hadn't changed much from the days when they'd been unable to study in the same room without erupting in giggles every five minutes. Rosie was just as exuberant as ever, but Amanda felt as if the fun had been drained out of her in the last year and a half. No, she wasn't here for the skiing or the scenery or the climbing or the clear, clean air. She was here to get her self back on track. To find what she'd lost back there in Chicago's Memorial Hospital—trust, hope, and a fresh outlook on life. Did Rosie know all that? If she did, she'd never let on.

"But if the doctor says he should be hospitalized, he must still be in pretty bad shape," Amanda said, getting back to the subject of the patient.

"Oh, yes." Rose looked over the papers on her desk. "I'd say so. He's pretty much immobilized and has a chest tube insertion."

"No wonder the doctor doesn't want him to leave the hospital. When was the accident?" Amanda asked.

"A week ago. And it's been chaotic in our little hospital ever since. Friends, relatives…"

"Well, that's normal."

"Friends, relatives flying in from all over the globe? Ignoring the posted visiting hours? Partying in the hall? Is that normal? Not here it isn't. Not to mention catered meals, loud music coming from his room. Definitely not normal. Oh, yes, we have the occasional hot dogger who busts out of his room and tries to go back up to the slopes as soon as he's conscious, but this is different. This guy happens to be a sheik. He has money and money talks."

"A sheik as in desert tents, harems and camels?" Amanda asked.

"A sheik as in oil money, private school education, and stunning good looks, too, according to the nurses at the hospital. I haven't seen him myself, just talked to him on the phone." Rosie sighed. "That was enough."

"What do you mean?"

"I mean, the man knows what he wants and he wants to go home. He doesn't seem to realize how sick he really is. That he's lucky to be allowed to leave the hospital so soon. Their ski cabin is not what you or I would call a cabin. It's a house on the lake which is big enough to house the entire extended family of sheiks and then some. According to family members, there's a live-in housekeeper and a suite with a private entrance available for the nurse. Let's hope the man has come to his senses and realizes he can't go back to San Francisco with a chest tube between his ribs."

"Do I have a choice in this?" Amanda asked. Being a private duty nurse to a guy like that could be a problem. A different kind of problem than the one she left behind, but still...

"Of course," Rosie assured her. "You could go right

into Intensive Care at the hospital. They're always short-handed and I'm sure they'd love to have you.''

''And the sheik?''

''I told him I'd do what I could. If I can't find anybody, and it can't be just anybody, he'll have to stay in the hospital.''

Amanda nodded.

''Why don't you go by the hospital,'' Rosie suggested. ''You'll want to see it anyway. It's nothing compared to St. Vincent's in Chicago, but we're proud of it. A few years ago we had to take the long drive to the hospital at the South Shore just to have a baby or an X ray. The whole town got together to raise the money to build the hospital. Pop in and take a look at our boy the sheik and see what you think. And don't forget dinner tonight at our house.''

Amanda stood and put her jacket on. ''I can't keep imposing on you, Rosie,'' she said. ''You've already done so much.''

Rosie came around her desk and hugged her friend. ''You are *not* imposing. I'm just so glad to have you here. Of all my friends…well, let's just say I don't have that many anymore what with my life these days. You're the best. You always were. I've never known anybody I could talk to like you. We shared so much. I've missed that. You knew all my secrets and you kept them. I didn't know how rare that was, now I do.'' Rosie stepped back and wiped a tear from her eye with the back of her hand. ''Now look what you've done. You've made me get all emotional.''

''Me, too,'' Amanda confessed. Her lower lip quivered. A friend as good as Rosie was hard to find. Maybe that was why she'd never found another one. Maybe that was why she was here, because everyone was only allowed one best friend. If so, was it right to keep a secret from your best friend, even now, after being apart for so long? If it was the biggest secret of your life and the most shameful, it was. It had to be.

"Six o'clock," Rosie said firmly. "My au pair is making fondue. And don't worry. If the sheik is obnoxious, the hell with him."

With those words ringing in her ears, Amanda drove slowly down the main street toward the hospital, passing restaurants and motels that catered to the ski crowd, including the one where she was staying. Rosie had invited her to stay with her, but Amanda wanted her own space. Even if it was only a room. It would do until she found an apartment.

The hospital was located one mile outside of town. It was small, smaller than she'd imagined. But then she was used to the big-city atmosphere of St. Vincent's Hospital on Chicago's north side with its adjoining medical school. Just its parking garage was ten times the size of this whole hospital. Amanda reminded herself that the town had built the hospital because they'd wanted it so badly. She also reminded herself she was looking for a change. It looked as if she was going to get it. Had she let Rosie's natural enthusiasm delude her into thinking she could really be happy in a small mountain town full of rabid outdoor types?

Happy? What was that? All she asked was that she not be depressed. That she stop thinking about the past. That she not cry herself to sleep at night and dream about the one person she wanted most of all to forget. If she could achieve that much then she'd be content. Contentment was her goal. Only that. She had a long way to go just to get there.

As she walked into the lobby she noted a few patients

in wheelchairs who glanced at her with curiosity and a lady in a hospital gown demanding something from the receptionist. The familiar smell of disinfectant was in the air causing her to feel apprehensive. Amanda had a sinking feeling in the pit of her stomach. While she had never considered escaping from caregiving, from doctors and nurses, or from the gossip and the back biting in a hospital, she had thought she could possibly escape from her own fears and her own mistakes. She'd needed a change, but maybe this was not the place for the change. She had to get away from Chicago, but maybe she'd come too far. Or not far enough. She tried to imagine working here, but she couldn't.

Instead of joining the hospital staff, maybe this sheik business was the way to go. It was a short-term job, no breach of contract if this wasn't the right place for her. No obligations. The more she thought of it, the better it sounded.

Amanda told the receptionist whose name tag said Carrie who she was.

"You're the nurse from Chicago," Carrie said with a friendly smile. "How do you like it here?"

"It's…it's beautiful. I've never seen the Sierras before."

"People call it paradise," she said modestly. "You gonna take the job with the sheik?"

"I don't know."

"He's a handful. Cute, though. He doesn't like being laid up, I can tell you. No patience. None whatsoever." Carrie turned to the nurse's aide who stopped to say hello and be introduced to the new nurse. "Am I right, Amy? The sheik in 34C. Isn't he something else? Phone calls, visitors, flowers, people coming and going. But nothing seems to cheer him up. He's got everything money can buy, but that's not what he wants. He wants to walk out of here and he wants to leave today. Determined, wouldn't you say, Amy?''

Amy agreed wholeheartedly. Amanda had had all kinds of patients, passive and easygoing, rich or indigent, willful, determined and obstinate. Some had visitors, some got flowers. Some were ignored. Those were the sad cases. It seemed to her the determined, stubborn types got well the fastest. It wasn't based on anything scientific, it was just her observation. Someday she'd do a study on personality types and healing.

''You won't believe this guy,'' Carrie continued enthusiastically. ''I don't think I've seen him smile once. 'Course maybe I wouldn't be smiling, either, with a tube between my ribs and a broken ankle. I felt so sorry for him I let him talk me into driving into town to get him the San Francisco newspaper and a pizza after I finished my shift. Says he can't stand hospital food. I asked him, Well, who can? So he shrugs and says then buy enough for the whole floor. So I did after I checked with Dietary to see if it was okay. What could I say when he looked at me with those big brown eyes? Oh, he's irresistible, if you like the long-suffering, rich, handsome type who use their charm to get their own way.'' She giggled and waved her hand toward the hallway to her right. ''Room 34C. Right down the hall.''

The more Amanda heard about the sheik the more she was sure he was just the type she'd have no trouble resisting at all. The type who used his money and influence to get more attention from an overworked staff. Not that Carrie seemed to mind, still…

Room 34C was almost dark. Only a small amount of late-afternoon sun filtered through the slanted blinds. A small table lamp glowed softly. Amanda didn't expect anyone stuck in the hospital with multiple injuries to radiate happiness, but she didn't expect such sadness. The somber expression on the face of the man in the bed and the sorrow in his deep dark eyes gave no hint of the man she'd heard about—the man possessed with only one thought, to get out of there or the extravagant rich guy who'd sent out for pizza for the whole floor.

She stood there in the doorway of his private room for a long moment studying him before he noticed her. He had a bandage around his forehead that contrasted with his dark hair. One large bandaged foot was propped up at the end of his bed. There were no visitors, no blaring TV as from the other rooms, no music, nothing. He was sitting up in bed staring straight ahead, lost in thought or perhaps semiconscious or in pain. Where were the visitors, the family, the friends?

At last he turned his head and saw her. He stared at her for at least as long as she'd stared at him. Steadily, unblinking. She wasn't prepared for this. She was there to evaluate him, but she had the feeling he'd turned the tables on her. She balled her hands into fists. Her fingers were icy. What was he thinking? What was going on behind that bandaged forehead, what emotion lurked in the depths of those eyes?

She ought to say something. Introduce herself. Ask how he was. But she couldn't speak. Her lips wouldn't move, her throat was clogged. She told herself he was just a patient like every other patient she'd seen before. If she took him on he'd be just another patient to assess, evaluate, change bandages, check blood pressure, breathing, etc., etc. But standing there locked in this endless, wordless gaze with him, she knew deep down he was not like any other patient she'd ever had.

He was the one who finally broke the silence.

"Who are you?" he asked. His voice was deep and uneven. In the silence of the room it reverberated and struck a chord in her soul. His eyes narrowed. Before she could answer, he continued. "Don't just stand there. Get in here. Open the blinds so I can see you."

Like a mindless robot, she walked to the window and opened the blinds just slightly. He had the manner of one who gave orders and was used to having them obeyed. But she was not used to taking orders from patients and she wasn't about to start now. She straightened her shoulders and found her voice. Not only her voice but her professional demeanor.

"I'm Amanda Reston. I'm a nurse."

"Rahman Harun," he said. "Forgive me for not getting up. May I say without insulting you or your profession that you don't look like a nurse. Much too young. Much too beautiful."

There it was. The so-called charm she'd expected. Next he'd tell her he was ready to go home and would she call a cab. If not, then he'd ask her to run into town for a six-pack and a hamburger. If he did, he'd soon find out she was not a messenger girl.

"I'm not on duty," she said stiffly. If she was going to work for him, which was not at all certain at this point, she'd have to establish that she was in charge. That she could not be used or manipulated. That if he wanted to get well, he'd do what she said. She was a professional and she was accustomed to respect. At least from her patients.

"So what brings you by, Nurse Reston?" he said, his voice husky and breathless. "To see what a sheik looks like? To watch how the mighty have fallen?" He choked on a mirthless laugh and reached for a glass of water. She automatically handed it to him. He wrapped his blunt fingers around hers. Amanda felt a shock travel up her arm. Despite the need to remain professional, she almost dropped the glass. He was breathing hard. So was she.

"Are you okay?" she asked, setting the glass firmly in his hand. She should have asked herself the same question.

"I'm fine. Just great." He gulped some water and pointed to the foot of his bed. "Read my chart there if you don't believe me. Don't be fooled by this bandage on my head, or the torn ligament in my ankle or that tube between my ribs. I'm really fine. So fine I'm going home as soon as I can get a...hey, that's you, isn't it? You're the hotshot nurse who's going to go home with me.

"I heard all about you. They thought I was asleep, but I wasn't. Ten years in ICU as a trauma nurse. I thought you'd be about fifty pounds heavier, have gray hair and thick ankles." He tilted his head to one side to get a better look at her. His gaze lingered on the contours of her lower body under her stretch pants. It was so intense Amanda felt her knees shake. She blushed and shifted her weight from one leg to the other, wishing she'd never come.

She didn't want to take on a patient who affected her this way. She told herself he was just checking her out the way she was evaluating him. After all, he was the one who'd be hiring her. He had a right to pick someone older with more experience and thicker ankles if that's what he wanted. Why she was reacting like a juvenile instead of a mature woman, she didn't know.

"From what I can see, I've lucked out, for once. So let's go, Amanda Reston." He swung his good leg over the side of the bed and reached for the buzzer to summon the nurse.

"Wait a minute, wait a minute," Amanda said, lifting his leg back onto the bed. "You haven't been discharged yet and I haven't said I'd take the job. I'm new here in town. I just got here and I don't know what my options are. And I'm not sure I'd be right for you."

She was not going to let the sheik call the shots or make her feel like a sex object any more than she'd let an arrogant surgeon do those things. She had not jumped out of the frying pan in Chicago into the fire in this mountain paradise. If she took the job, it would be her decision. She wouldn't be pressured or charmed. Sure, he was handsome and determined, but that wasn't enough to sell her on the idea of taking him on. Just the reverse. She didn't need to be around a man who affected her like this one did without even trying.

He glared at her. "Options. You've got options. Good for you. I had options a few days ago, but as of now, I'm fresh out What's all this about being right for me? It's just a job, Nurse Reston. I can't afford to be choosy. If I don't get a private-duty nurse, I have to stay here." He gazed around at the walls as if the room were a prison. To him, it probably was.

Rather than debate the merits of hospital accommodations, she changed the subject. "How did it happen?" she asked.

"The accident? The usual. I was taking a last run and I lost control and rolled down the hill. Do you ski?"

Amanda shook her head.

"It's a great sport. There's nothing like it. The speed, the wind in your face, the mountains…" For a brief moment there was a half smile on his craggy face. She caught a glimpse of what he might have been before the accident, only a short time ago. She felt a pang of sympathy mingled with curiosity. This wouldn't do, it wouldn't do at all. She had to keep her professional distance. But she couldn't help wondering, what was he like before it happened? She'd never know.

"Until you fall and puncture your lung," she concluded dryly.

"Do you believe in accidents?"

"Of course."

"I don't. I believe you get what you deserve. I was pushing the envelope. I was asking for it, just like..." He took a shallow breath, leaned forward and pinned her with his gaze. "It was my fault. Whatever happened was because of what I did. I was careless. So I'm paying the price for my so-called accident. That's the way it should be. This accident did not happen by chance. It happened for a reason." He put so much emphasis on every word of that last sentence, it seemed to exhaust him. He let his head fall back on the pillow and closed his eyes. His forehead was furrowed.

Concerned, Amanda sat on a stool by the bed and took his pulse. It was fast but strong. Before she could remove her hand, Rahman grabbed it with his other hand. For someone so badly injured, he had surprising strength.

"Cold hands," he murmured, his eyes drifting open and then shut again. "We have a saying in Arabic, 'Cold hands mean warm heart.'" His voice faded to a whisper. "Is that true? Is your heart warm, Amanda?"

Had he really said that, or had she just imagined it? In any case, it was fortunate the question didn't require an answer, because she couldn't have articulated one. For the second time this afternoon she was speechless. Luckily no one was taking her pulse because she felt it speed up uncontrollably. What on earth was wrong with

her? It must be the altitude. That was it. Some people
got dizzy, others got breathless or had an increased heart
rate. Although she'd been in the mountains for two days
with no ill effects, she was suddenly in the throes of
some kind of altitude sickness. Or...

In any case, whether she had a warm heart or not was
none of the sheik's business. Amanda knew she ought
to leave. She'd seen enough and heard enough. More
than enough. But though he appeared to have dropped
off into semiconsciousness, he was still holding her hand
so tightly that she couldn't pull it away. Couldn't or
wouldn't? She sat there for a long moment, mesmerized
by the scent of spring flowers from the bouquets in
vases, the pattern of sunlight on the bed, the warmth of
his hand in hers. A current of energy seemed to flow
from her to him and back again. She didn't want to
move, didn't want to leave. But of course she had to.

No. She couldn't do it. Couldn't be his nurse.
Couldn't take care of him twenty-four hours a day.
Couldn't live in his ski cabin. She'd come here for a
break. She could not afford one bit of emotional involve-
ment with anyone. Not with a doctor, not with a patient.
All she wanted was to live quietly and simply. Alone.
To leave her work at the end of the day and not take it
home with her. Underneath the scent of freesias and hy-
acinths, she smelled danger in this room. A threat to her
new life and the serenity she was looking for. Inside her
chest she felt her heart bang against her ribs. It felt like
fear. She'd tell Rosie tonight she couldn't do it. Rosie
would understand.

When Amanda finally pulled her hand loose from
Rahman's grasp, he gave a ragged sigh and mumbled
something she couldn't understand about being sorry.
Glancing back toward him as she tiptoed to the door,

she nearly ran into the tall figure standing in the doorway. She gasped in surprise. The man was the mirror image of the sheik in the bed. Or what Rahman would look like if he was healthy. Had she gone crazy? Was she seeing double?

"You must be the nurse," he said. "I'm Rafik, Rahman's brother. Can I have a word with you?"

"Of course," she said softly and they walked down the hall to the lounge together while she practiced what she would say to him.

I'm not going to take the job. I can't take care of your brother. It has nothing to do with him and everything to do with me. I'm in recovery, too. Some things I can handle. Some things I can't. A man like your brother falls into the latter category. I'm sorry, but I'm not the right person for the job.

Chapter Two

"**W**ell, what did you think?" Rosie asked the minute Amanda walked into her friend's kitchen where the fondue was bubbling on the stove and the air was filled with the rich aroma of cheese and kirsch.

"He's in bad shape," Amanda said, hanging her jacket on a hook near the door.

Rosie nodded and handed her friend a glass of white wine.

"More than you can manage? Worse than you thought?"

"Yes. No. I don't know." What could she say? How to explain that after all these years of professional nursing, a patient had touched her somewhere that was off limits. And that she was still reeling from the shock.

At that moment, Rosie's husband Jake burst in the back door. "Welcome to California, Amanda. I hope you're here to stay." His face was ruddy, his voice was booming. Amanda had only met him once, at their wedding back in Chicago, Rosie's hometown, but he greeted her with a welcoming hug as if he was as glad to see her as his wife was. Then he kissed Rosie as if he hadn't seen her for weeks instead of hours and Amanda felt a pang of most unbecoming envy. Their affection for each other was out in the open for all to see. The way it should be. No sneaking around. Hiding from sight. Fearing being caught. It was clear they'd forged solid, unbreakable ties that nothing could separate.

Overriding the envy was happiness for her friend. When Rosie alluded to her secrets, Amanda knew they weren't all happy ones. Rosie had put in her time, had had her share of heartbreak and disappointment. What was it Rahman had said he believed? ''You get what you deserve.'' Was that true? Did Amanda deserve what she'd gotten? To have her heart broken? She hoped not. If she had, she had turned over a new leaf in a new place. Never again would a man take advantage of her. Never again would she be fooled into trusting a man.

If Amanda was envious at meeting Rosie's husband, she was more so when she saw the three-year-old twin girls, Sara and Nora. She got down on her knees and put an arm around each one of them. This was certainly her day for twins, she thought. Unlike Rahman and his brother Rafik, these two were identical in energy, charm and looks. Over their mother's protests, the girls dragged Amanda to their room to show her their beds, their dolls, their toy house, their pet hamster and their books. They asked her a million questions.

They climbed into her lap, they combed her hair with their Barbie doll's tiny comb and brush. Amanda felt a cold lump in her chest she didn't know was there start to melt away. Felt the tension of the day fade as fast as the sun set behind the mountains. She could have gladly stayed there all evening, playing pretend games. Pre-

tending that these were her children, this was her life.
Pretending she didn't have a tough job ahead of her.

Amanda didn't know what had happened to her. She'd
never longed for children the way Rosie had. But now
that she'd seen these two, now that they were so close
she could smell their baby shampoo, feel their soft skin
and hear their little voices chatter away, she'd had a
vision, an epiphany. This is what it could be like, should
be like. Only it wasn't.

She came back to earth with a thud. She was pretending just like the children. She'd had quite a day. First,
she was still in shock, coming to a small mountain community from a big city only a few days ago. Second, she
was in culture shock from meeting the twin sheiks. One
intense, demanding, difficult, and maddeningly attractive
despite everything. The other kind and persuasive. Just
as good-looking, but there was no tension between them.
No electric current flowed between them the way it had
between Rahman and herself. Of course, if it wasn't the
altitude that caused her reaction to Rahman, it could be
a reaction to what she'd left behind, to the man who'd
deceived her. Amanda knew she was vulnerable. She
knew her heart had been ripped out of her chest and
broken in two. She needed time to heal, just like Rahman
did. It didn't take a brain surgeon to tell her that.

When the au pair came to retrieve the little girls for
their baths, they kissed Amanda good-night and she re-
luctantly went back to the kitchen to help Rosie toss the
salad.

"The girls are crazy about you," Rosie said as the
three of them sat down at the candlelit dining room table.

"It's mutual," Amanda said. "I'm gaga over them.
They're the cutest things I've ever seen."

"Thank you," Rosie said with a proud smile. "Now

have some fondue and then tell us what happened with the sheik.''

''I met him and I decided I couldn't do it,'' she said.

''Why, what did he say? How did he act?'' Rosie asked.

''Just the way I'd expected. Impatient, arrogant, demanding. I told myself life is too short to spend it on somebody like that.''

''Of course he's sick,'' Rosie interjected. ''Being sick brings out the worst in anyone.''

''I know. I know. I tried to make allowances for that. He has every right to be cranky. He's obviously in pain. He's frustrated. He's used to being in charge. Suddenly he's immobilized. Has to ring a bell when he wants something. It's difficult. It's humiliating.'' As she said the words she pictured the man in the bed, his gaze haunting her even now, hours later. She remembered the way he held her hand and she held his.

''Why do I get the feeling you're going to say 'but...?''' Rosie asked with a smile.

''But he's a sheik,'' Amanda reiterated. ''I don't know for sure, but I have the feeling the traits I saw today will be there when he gets well. I suspect that he's spoiled and that he's always gotten everything he's ever wanted.'' If so, then why the sad look when he thought no one was looking? Maybe he hadn't really gotten everything he'd ever wanted. ''I've dealt with a lot of difficult patients, but this man...''

''He got to you, didn't he?'' Rosie asked, her forehead puckered in a frown. ''That's not like you. Not like the old cool and calm Amanda. You were such a natural in the trauma center. Nothing rattled you. But this guy rattled you, I can tell. How come?''

''Maybe I felt sorry for him and I didn't want to.''

Maybe I was attracted to him and I didn't want to be. "I don't know."

Amanda played over their conversation as she ate her salad. Why had Rahman gotten to her? Why had she reacted so strongly? She'd had good-looking male patients before. Patients who flirted with her and who tried to make passes at her from their hospital beds. She'd been able to rebuff them pleasantly and firmly and that was the end of it. Rahman hadn't even really flirted with her.

"Sorry," Amanda said jolted out of her reverie. "Did you ask me something?"

"I gather you've decided not to take his case then," Rosie said.

"No, despite what I said, I'm going to do it."

"What?" Rosie's mouth fell open in surprise.

"A funny thing happened on my way out of Rahman's room. I ran into Rafik. That's the sheik's twin brother. He's everything Rahman isn't. He's very nice and low-key and thoughtful. He asked if he could talk to me and we went to the lounge where I told him I couldn't take the case.

"He said he understood but asked me to think it over. Maybe if I saw the place... So we drove to the ski 'cabin' as you call it. And you're right, it's a beautiful house, all done in natural wood and stone with a spectacular view of the lake. They've ordered every kind of equipment you can think of for his recovery. A veritable rehab unit right there on the lake with a year-round housekeeper who is a great cook, if the smells coming from the kitchen are any indication.

"I met the whole family, his brother's wife, his cousin, his wife and a few others I'm not sure who they were. They convinced me to take on Rahman. They said he hasn't been himself lately. It's not just his accident. It's other things, too. Apparently he's not only hurting physically, he's also hurting emotionally. They didn't say what the other things were. I suppose it's none of my business.''

"So they talked you into it," Rosie said. "I hope it works out."

"So do I because the die is cast. The family is all leaving town to go back to San Francisco now that they've found me.''

"I hope they know how lucky they are," Rosie said emphatically.

"They're definitely making it worth my while," Amanda admitted. "I'm not just doing it out of the goodness of my heart. They've offered me a lot of money and I get to live in that gorgeous house." That didn't change the fact that she was risking her newfound serenity. That she wasn't at all sure it was the right thing to do.

"When will the hospital discharge him?" Rosie asked.

"I'll talk to the doctor tomorrow. The house isn't quite ready yet. Needless to say Rahman is impatient."

"You can ask Doc Flanders about his discharge," Rosie said. "I'm so glad this has worked out. I hope…well I hope I haven't led you astray."

"It's too soon to say it's worked out, but whatever happens, it was my decision. You never pressured me." Amanda tried to sound calm and confident, but in fact her stomach did flip-flops at the thought of staying under the same roof as the sheik. Being with him night and day. Hearing him moan in his sleep. Administering his medicine round the clock. Sitting by the side of his bed monitoring his lung capacity, testing him for complications or distress.

She knew she could help him recover. But what would happen to her in the process? For Rahman to get well, she would need his help. He had to make the effort. Did he have the drive, the will to help her help him? She kept seeing his face, his hollow eyes. She kept hearing his deep voice tell her that things happened for a reason. If Rahman didn't believe he deserved to recover, he might not.

The next day, Amanda was back at the hospital. After talking to the doctor and Rahman's family, it was decided to release him after the house was renovated and at least partly ready for him. In addition to what had already been done, workmen had been dispatched to install ramps for Rahman's wheelchair and a hospital bed was to be installed in a bedroom on the first floor.

Amanda should have been flattered the doctor had so much faith in her that he'd consider discharging Rahman so soon. Of course, Dr. Flanders may have had other motives for getting rid of the patient who was consistently asking the nurses for something. She also should have been flattered that Rahman's family had placed their confidence in her. But they had been desperate and had little choice. Even if Amanda should have been flattered, she wasn't.

All she felt was cold on the outside and hollow on the inside. She was worried. Worried about this kind of heavy-duty nursing. Worried about their nurse-patient relationship. One-on-one contact with a man who'd had such a strange effect on her. She told herself she was being overly sensitive. He was just another patient. To be treated like all her other patients. Amanda repeated it to herself until it had sunk in.

She looked at herself in the mirror in the hospital rest-room. She didn't look nervous. She'd had years of prac-tice of not showing emotion in front of her patients. Sometimes she had kept this mask on in her private life as well. Today, she needed it more than ever. Nobody wanted a nurse who had doubts about her job. She prac-ticed a bright smile. Not bad for someone who wanted to run out the front door and take the first plane back to Chicago. *From the frying pan into the fire* was the phrase that kept running through her mind.

Amanda kept the smile pasted on her face when she headed to Rahman's room. She thought he'd be de-lighted to be getting out so soon. He was far from it. She stood outside the room and listened to him rant and rave at his family.

"You're leaving? Everyone is leaving and going about their lives while I waste away here by myself? Transfer me to a hospital in San Francisco," he shouted. Only his shout came out like a wheeze. "I'm not staying here."

A woman spoke in a soft lightly accented voice. "Rahman," she said. "Calm down. You're in no con-dition to travel. You know that. As soon as you are, you can come home. Everything is arranged. The house is being set up and we have hired you a wonderful nurse. We met her yesterday and we were very impressed. She's been highly recommended."

"Highly recommended by who? The doctors at this hospital? They'll do anything to get rid of me. That's fine with me. I want to leave. I don't need some special nurse. How do they know what I need? Get me out of this place. I'm going home. And I don't mean the ski cabin."

A gruff-voiced older man spoke next. "You can't go

back to the city. Not yet. You're much too sick. You've had a serious accident. You're lucky to be alive.''

"Lucky? You think I'm lucky? Have you ever been confined to a bed all hours of the day except to hobble to the bathroom? Had to take a stack of pills just to keep the pain from taking over? To feel like hell all the time anyway? To think you're losing your mind as well as the use of your legs. Not to be able to get enough air to breathe? You call that lucky?''

"Rahman!" the woman said in a voice full of indignation.

"Sorry, Father," Rahman said, in a subdued tone.

Amanda stood outside the door wishing she hadn't heard all that. She had thought everything was in order. She had thought he was reconciled to staying at the ski cabin. She had thought he'd be grateful to his family. What had caused this outburst? He sounded like a spoiled brat. Should she sneak away and pretend she'd never heard anything at all? As she was pondering her choices, Rahman's twin brother came out and greeted her.

"I assume you heard all that," he said with a grim look.

"I'm afraid so.''

"He doesn't mean it. He's upset because we're leaving.''

She gave him her best hospital smile, totally insincere and hoped he wouldn't notice. "It's understandable," she said. But it certainly wasn't a good way to start this job. As if she hadn't been worried enough. Now she knew how desperately Rahman didn't want to be there, didn't want to be left behind, and didn't want to have her for his nurse. It hurt more than it should, even though she knew enough not to take it personally. She was being ridiculous and far too sensitive. She knew perfectly well how he was feeling—helpless, insecure, and in real pain.

"Good. I'm glad you understand," his brother said.

"I'll come back later," Amanda said. "When things have calmed down."

His room was empty. His family had finally left to go to dinner at some lakeside restaurant. Rahman wanted them to stay, but he was also glad to see them leave. He loved them but he couldn't stand to be around them. They were driving him crazy with their lectures and their orders. But without them he was unbearably lonely. He sometimes felt he was losing his mind just when he needed it the most. It must be the medicine that made him so ambivalent. In the past, he had been able to pretty much do whatever he wanted. Now he had to rely on others for everything and it was not a good feeling. He'd always had an strong independent streak. He'd never minded being alone because he knew Rafik was around and Lisa and the rest of his family.

But now…he had no one. Even his twin brother, his closest friend in the world, didn't seem to understand what he was going through. Ever since Rafik's marriage there had been a gap between them. Now more than ever. He saw the way Rafik looked at him, the one person who ought to sympathize was baffled and annoyed by his behavior.

Rahman watched the sun set behind the mountains with heavy-lidded eyes. It was hard to believe he'd been on top of those mountains only days ago. How many days? He didn't know. The days and nights blended together. Whenever he fell asleep, someone came in and woke him up to take his temperature or give him some medicine. The lights in the hall were on all day and all night. He didn't know which was which. Nurses came and went. He couldn't keep them straight.

Except for the one called Amanda. The one who was going to go home with him, no matter how much he objected. She was different. He could never mistake her for the others. She radiated calm and serenity and excited him at the same time.

Why didn't she wear white like the other nurses? She wore those stretch pants over a pair of incredible legs. What would she wear when she was taking care of him? His mind conjured up all kinds of pictures. Amanda in a starchy white dress, Amanda in a blue turtleneck sweater that matched her eyes and showed off her curves. He felt his pulse speed up. What would happen to his vital signs when she was around 24/7?

He didn't want her.

He hated the idea of a young attractive nurse taking care of him as if he were a baby. It was going to be humiliating to have her giving him his food and his medicine and telling him what to do and him being in no condition to resist. If he had to have a woman take care of him, she should at least be old and ugly. How hard could it be to find an old and ugly nurse? How hard could it be to hire a helicopter to airlift him out of here and back to the city? His family obviously hadn't tried very hard. They didn't know it, and he wasn't going to tell them, but if he spent much time with Amanda he was going to want things he couldn't have.

He was going to avoid all future entanglements with women. No more thrill-seekers like Lisa and especially no women like Amanda, a woman whose life was devoted to taking care of people. He didn't want to be taken care of. Not by anyone. He was through with women of any kind. He'd had his chance, then fate had intervened and taken away the most vibrant, exciting woman he'd ever met. There wouldn't be another like her. Destiny had decreed a life of loneliness for him and he'd damned well better get used to it.

He closed his eyes and his mind drifted. What was wrong with him? He kept seeing Amanda even though she wasn't there. Hallucinations, that's what it was. He remembered how she looked standing there in his doorway the first time he saw her. He thought he'd died and gone to heaven for one brief moment. He remembered falling asleep with her at his bedside and waking up without that groggy, drugged feeling. That was a good thing. But it would never happen again. He couldn't ask her to hold his hand every night at bedtime. Yes, he was sick, but that's not what nurses did. He kicked the metal bed frame with his good foot and winced. Damn this accident. Damn this little town and its hospital.

When he looked up she was standing in the doorway again. But was she really there? Or was it just another illusion? If she was real, he wished he'd had time to sit up and try to look alert, at least run his fingers through his hair. He hated it when he saw pity in the nurses' eyes. That was one good thing about her, there was no pity in her eyes. There was something else, but he didn't know what to call it.

"Don't you ever knock?" he growled.

"I didn't want to wake you," she said.

"I wasn't asleep," he said.

"How are you feeling?"

"You're the nurse. You know everything. You tell me."

"You have a healthy attitude," she said.

"Is that what you call it?"

"I have a theory that the most obnoxious patients, the

ones who fight back are the ones who get well the fastest."

"You think I'm obnoxious?"

"I think your behavior is."

His mouth twisted in a wry smile. "You could be right." Rahman looked her over for a long moment. Amanda was wearing a blue turtleneck sweater and dark wool pants, almost exactly what he'd pictured her in. He felt a surge of sexual awareness rocket through his body. It caught him by surprise. He thought his responses were all numb. He didn't expect to feel anything ever again. But there it was.

Even though he couldn't do anything about it, it was a good sign. At least that part of him was still functional. For all the good it did him. In any case it was something to be celebrated. Or was it? Would it just lead to more frustration? One more thing he couldn't do? "Come in and sit down," he said. "Is this a social call or professional?"

"Both." She sat on the little stool next to his bed. Just where she was the last time she was here. "I know how you feel about staying here in town and having me as your nurse."

"What are you, psychic?" He told himself she was bluffing. She couldn't possibly know that she turned him on and that was the real reason he didn't want her around, didn't trust himself with her around, didn't want to be tempted when he couldn't perform and was through with women for good, could she?

"I was standing outside the door when you were talking to your family. When you insisted they take you back with them and you said you didn't need me."

"I don't remember that. I must have been delirious. Of course I need you. My family thinks you're the greatest. Who am I to disagree?'' What else could he say? He'd been trained all his life in etiquette and hospitality. Though he and his brother had been sent to boarding school in the U.S., his upbringing had been traditional. His parents had instilled in him the values of their family and their country such as loyalty and responsibility. He hadn't always lived up to those values as his father often had occasion to remind him.

What possible reason could he give for objecting to her? That she was too attractive, too sexy in a subdued kind of way that got to him? That he didn't trust himself around her? That he didn't want to be humiliated around her? That he preferred to get well on his own without her watching and monitoring him every step of the way? No, he was resigned to staying here and having her around night and day. There was nothing he could do about it.

"Well, if you're sure…" she said.

"What about you? Why in hell would you want to take me on with my obnoxious attitude? Don't you have anything better to do?"

"I was looking for a challenge."

"Hah. Well, sweetheart, you've got one."

She pressed her lips together and her cheeks flushed. He'd said something to annoy her.

"You can call me Amanda or Nurse Reston but you can't call me sweetheart. I'm a professional."

So that was it. How could she know that being told he couldn't do something was all the incentive he needed to do it anyway? "Of course you are, sweetheart," he said.

Her eyes flashed. Damn, she was cute when she was mad. It only encouraged him to see what else he could say to bring color to her cheeks and sparkle to her eyes.

"Sorry," he said. But he wasn't and she knew it.

"I hear you don't like hospital food. Can I bring you something from town? I'm on my way to dinner."

"Alone?"

"Does it matter?" she asked.

"It was just a question. You're not required to answer. But since we're going to be living together, I don't think we should have any secrets from each other." As soon as he said those words, he regretted them. While he was intensely curious about her, he had no intention of sharing any of his secrets with her.

"I don't agree. I think we need to establish a professional relationship. I believe I already told you that I'm new in town and therefore I will be eating alone tonight at the Japanese restaurant."

"Sorry," he said. "I was out of line. It's none of my business who you eat with. If you really don't mind, you could bring me something. Anything would be better than the slop they serve here."

"All right."

Even though it was none of his business who she ate with or whether she was married or engaged or whatever, he thought it was a good sign she was eating alone. What husband or fiancé in his right mind would let her go by herself to a new town and be forced to eat alone? He certainly wouldn't. Not that it mattered whether she was available or not. He wasn't. He had sworn off women after Lisa's accident. He would never take on the responsibility of a woman again. He would never set himself up to suffer like that again.

She nodded and stood up. "I'll tell the nurses you don't want a dinner tray and I'll be back in an hour or so."

"This is embarrassing. I don't have any money.

They've taken away my ring and my watch and my wallet. But I'm good for it.''

She smiled. And what a smile. It warmed him more than all those hot compresses the therapist put on his hip. ''I'm sure you are,'' she said.

''You ought to do that more often,'' he said.

''What, go out for Japanese food?''

''Smile.''

She stopped at the door and stared at him for a long thoughtful moment. Her smile faded. He would have given everything in his wallet to know what she was thinking. Their eyes met and held for a long time. In the background doctors were being paged. Carts were clattering down the hall. All the sounds that usually irritated him. Now he scarcely heard them. What or who had taken away her smile? Who or what could bring it back? A long time ago, when he was a man-about-town, he'd have considered it his personal challenge. But now he didn't know if he had what it took.

''I'll think about it,'' she said finally and then she was gone. The room was empty again.

She did think about it. While all around her at various tables, apple-cheeked skiers in casual après-ski clothes laughed and talked and traded stories of what happened on the slopes that day, Amanda thought about the reason she didn't smile much anymore. She thought how odd it was that a stranger had to point it out. Someone who didn't know her. If he knew what had happened he would have told her she'd been a fool. He wasn't worth suffering over. But Rahman didn't know and she was not going to tell. There were secrets she didn't intend to share with anyone, least of all him.

When she came back to the hospital with a foam box

in a white paper bag from the restaurant in her hand she was stopped by the night nurse who informed her stiffly that visiting hours were over.

Amanda explained who she was and where she was going and got a shrug and a disapproving look in return.

"That man," the nurse said huffily, "has been pushing his buzzer for the last hour. He wanted a phone, a TV, a pain pill and his wallet. I'm a nurse, not a servant. I'm all alone here on this floor. He's not the only patient in this hospital. Who does he think he is anyway?"

Amanda bit back an angry retort. She should have hurried back. It was her fault he was left alone without the care he needed. She usually sympathized with nurses. She knew some patients were demanding. The sheik fell into that category at times. But she was also well aware that not all nurses were warm, sympathetic and caring. She tried to make allowances for burnout and fatigue, but this woman's attitude annoyed her. She almost blurted, "That's my patient you're talking about." She caught herself before she started to feel possessive about the sheik. She reminded herself he was just another patient. Just another sheik.

"You know he's probably hungry and he's tired and he's impatient," Amanda said. "I brought him something to eat."

"Dinner is at five," she sniffed. "The trays have come and gone."

"I know, that's why I..." Why bother to explain? This pinched-faced RN was of the old school that said everything had to be done by the book. Amanda felt bad she'd taken so long at dinner. She could imagine that lying there in bed watching the clock and waiting for dinner or a nurse to come could be agony. Though she'd never been hospitalized, she could certainly empathize.

But the nurse who looked at her with a steely gaze, obviously couldn't.

"I'm hungry, too," the nurse said. "And tired, and I have eight hours to go."

"I'm sorry. I know how it feels. I've worked a lot of night shifts." Amanda knew it was not easy working alone at night. Being responsible for all those patients. With a doctor a phone call away anything could happen and often did.

When the nurse pointedly picked up her pencil and went back to work filling out forms, Amanda hurried down the hall to find that Sheik Rahman Harun had fallen asleep. She stood next to his bed feeling deflated that she'd let him down. He'd been waiting for her and she hadn't made it back in time. The restaurant had been crowded and the service was slow. But he didn't know that. He just knew she hadn't shown up with his dinner as she'd promised.

She thought about waking him up, but she didn't. He needed his sleep. But he needed food, too. His cheek-bones were too prominent. She touched his shoulder. Smoothed his sheet. He frowned but he didn't wake up. She stood there for a long time trying to decide what to do. She hadn't realized how much she was looking forward to bringing him something and seeing him eat. Though she wasn't looking forward to hearing him make any more outrageous pronouncements like, "I don't think we should keep any secrets from each other." She was unaccountably disappointed. But was she disappointed for his sake or hers?

Amanda had no intention of spilling any of her secrets to him. If she did, she could just imagine what he'd think of her. She couldn't believe he'd share any secrets with her, either. Maybe he didn't have any. Although there was that issue of his suffering "emotionally." The remark he'd made was only to get her goat. At first he'd succeeded, now she realized she could talk back and he liked it. She liked it, too. If all went well, they might become friends. Friends. Was it possible to be a friend to a man like that? Time would tell.

He'd probably guessed she wasn't engaged or married. That was going to come out in the wash anyway. But that was the extent of the secrets she was sharing. Period.

Rahman mumbled something in his sleep. Amanda bent over his bed to listen but he didn't say any more. Only inches from his face, she brushed his dark thick hair back. She laid her hand on his forehead and kept it there. She told herself she would make him get well. She could do it. She knew she could. She willed him to sleep well, to sleep peacefully. She didn't know how long she stayed there. She only knew his breathing slowed and sounded normal.

Some time later she stood and found her leg muscles stiff and cramped. She walked slowly back to the nurse's station.

The nurse looked up at Amanda, glanced at her watch and frowned. Amanda set the bag with Rahman's dinner on the counter and told her it was for her. The woman looked startled, then suspicious, then she grudgingly accepted it. Amanda muttered, "you're welcome," to herself as she walked out the front door of the hospital feeling frustrated and sorry for the overworked nurse and even sorrier for Rahman.

She went back out into the cold mountain air and drove to her motel room, took a hot bath, lay on her queen-size bed and stared at the ceiling. Tomorrow night she'd be under the same roof as Rahman. Would he soon

turn her into a crabby, cranky nurse, annoyed and resentful every time he rang for her on the house intercom?
Or would she get too emotionally involved in nursing
him back to health? She couldn't let that happen. It was
better that she turn into a hag who barked orders. He
wasn't the only one who needed to be nursed back to
health.

As Rahman noticed, she didn't have a ready smile
except for rare occasions. But she'd come here to make
a fresh start. She'd do what she could within the bounds
of her profession and then send him back to San Francisco. And then what? What would she do? She didn't
see herself working at that hospital. Was it too small
after living and working in the fast lane? What about
Rosie and her life? How could Amanda have what she
had? A career, a husband and two adorable children.

She reminded herself that her goals were much more
modest than that. To fall asleep at night without dreaming of the arrogant doctor she'd left behind. To face each
day with some kind of enthusiasm instead of dread. To
regain the joy of helping others get well, to remember
why she'd become a nurse in the first place. If she could
accomplish that much, the trip would have been worthwhile.

She repeated these goals like a mantra and finally she
did fall asleep and she did not dream at all. That in itself
was a blessing and worth the price of the airline ticket.

The next day, there was so much activity at the hospital that Amanda didn't have time for second thoughts
about this unusual assignment. Rahman's family was
there and greeted her warmly. They hovered over him
in his room while Amanda conferred with doctors and
nurses, the pharmacist and the therapist. She spoke to
everyone in sight except for Rahman. She saw him only

briefly and only from a distance. She felt his eyes on
her. She saw him frown. She knew she owed him an
explanation about dinner. She wanted to apologize, but
she never got a chance. She went around and make appointments with the therapist and his doctor to come to
the house. An orderly pushed Rahman in his wheelchair
to the curb where an ambulance was waiting.

He wasn't happy to see the ambulance. She could tell
by the way he said, "Where's the car...? What the
hell..." in an angry voice that carried to where she was
standing at the glass doors to the hospital.

There was continued chaos at the house they called
their ski cabin. Workmen were building a ramp to the
back door like the one in front. The therapist was installing a massage table in the ballroom along with some
parallel bars. The housekeeper introduced herself and
said that dinner was at seven. Family members wandered
in and out, conferring with each other in hushed voices
as if they were at a wake.

Amanda and the orderly maneuvered Rahman into his
hospital bed in the room that used to be a study. Two
whole walls were lined with books, the other two had
windows with views of the lake and the mountains.
There was a fireplace with a fire already laid. How could
Rahman object to staying there? A view, a fireplace and
a housekeeper, too. But Amanda knew what he wanted.
What *every* patient wanted. To get back his old life, the
one he'd had before the accident.

Next to the study was an adjoining bathroom where a
plumber was installing bars in the shower stall and han-
dles in the tub. The walls were lined with Italian trav-
ertine marble and the room was large enough for an
entire Roman army to bathe. Everywhere there were
signs of wealth. Everywhere were signs of good taste.

Amanda had never seen a place quite like it. Rahman's family seemed to take it for granted.

As Amanda adjusted the height of his bed, Rahman grabbed her arm. "Where have you been?" he demanded. He was exhausted. He hadn't realized how tiring this move was going to be. For the first time he saw the folly of thinking he could be moved to the city. He felt like a fool for even suggesting it. Just coming this far had drained him of his energy, what little he'd had.

The chaos around the house was making him crazy and irritable. Rafik and his wife, Anne, came in to see how he was doing. He'd never been so aware of what he was missing than when he was around the couple. The way they looked at each other, communicating their feelings without words astounded him. So that was love. It made him realize he'd never been in love. He'd been in lust many times, and he'd been crazy about Lisa. But love?

Months after their wedding, Rafik and Anne were so obviously so madly in love it made him wonder how his brother had gotten so lucky. What had Rafik done to deserve that kind of happiness? Was it available to him, too? Not unless he cleaned up his act. They didn't say that to his face, but he knew that's what they were thinking. The truth was likely that such happiness was not in his destiny, not matter what he did.

"Where have you been?" he repeated.

"What do you mean?" Amanda said, taking his hand off her arm. "I've been around, doing what I needed to do."

"You're supposed to be around where I can see you. So I can call if I need you. That's what I'm paying you for." He knew how obnoxious he sounded, but he couldn't help it. He didn't have the strength to make the effort it took to be polite. He wanted everyone else to leave. He wanted peace and quiet and he wanted Amanda around where he could see her.

"I know why you're paying me," she assured him. "And I know what you need. Once your family leaves we'll set up a schedule. We'll decide on some rules and some boundaries."

"Boundaries?" he said. "Rules?" He didn't like the sound of that at all.

"Then you'll know what to expect."

He pressed his lips together in a hard line. He didn't like to remind her that *she* was working for *him*. She might remind him she wasn't a servant. She was a professional. She might threaten to leave.

"Right," he said tightly.

Her expression softened. "Look, I'm sorry about last night. When I got back with your dinner you were asleep."

"You owe me," he said. He'd never admit how disappointed he'd been when she didn't show up. How much it hurt to think of her out at a restaurant, laughing and talking and having a good time while he was stuck in a hospital room. Yes, she'd said she was eating alone, but his imagination had taken over when she didn't show up and he'd pictured her with other people, people who were healthy and entertaining. People who made her smile, even laugh. He'd imagined her forgetting all about him. Who could blame her? He wasn't healthy and he wasn't fun to be around. Not anymore.

"Yes, I know I owe you," Amanda said. "I'll make it up to you, I promise. You see this? You've got a bell here, ring it if you need somebody." She pressed down on it and it rang loud and clear. She really felt terrible about letting him down. It wasn't hard to feel sorry for yourself when you're lying flat on your back waiting...waiting. And nobody came.

"I don't need *somebody,* I need you."

She was startled at how strong his voice had suddenly become. It sent shock waves through her body. His eyes penetrated every layer of clothing right down to her bones. Her stomach felt like it had turned inside out. It must be because she'd skipped breakfast. She struggled for control. "I'll be around," she said as briskly as she could. "Or buzz me on the intercom and I'll come—as soon as I can."

"Like they did in the hospital? You'll have to do better than that."

"Look, Rahman..."

"Amanda, could you come here for a minute?" his brother said from the doorway.

"No, she couldn't, Rafik," Rahman called. "She's busy. Get your own nurse. This one is mine."

"You keep acting like a spoiled brat and you'll be lucky if she stays twenty-four hours," Rafik said with a grin. It was clear they were accustomed to teasing each other.

But Rahman was obviously not in the mood to be teased. He didn't return the grin, instead he glared at his twin. "May I remind you that I've been in an accident? That my head hurts, my ankle throbs and I have trouble breathing?"

"Sorry. I'm really sorry, Rahman, I know you're hurting, but look on the bright side. You're still alive. You've got a beautiful nurse. You've got yourself out of work for weeks, maybe months. With any luck, and if you do what Nurse Reston tells you, you might even ski again someday. Not that you were ever that good at it."

"I was a hell of a lot better than you were. You should have seen me on that last run…taking those moguls…no I guess you shouldn't have. Never mind."

Rahman's mouth turned down in a frown.

Rafik motioned silently to Amanda and she stepped softly out of the room following Rahman's brother to a pair of leather chairs in a corner of the room with the vaulted ceiling.

"I just wanted to say," Rafik said, sitting across from her, "how happy we are to have found you. If anyone can help my brother it's you."

"I'll do my best," she said. "But I can't do it by myself. He has to follow the doctor's orders whether he likes them or not and he has to really want to get well, physically and mentally."

"He does, I know he does. He's had a bad time of it but I think he'll come around. I know he's been down-right obnoxious lately. I hope he will treat you with respect. If he doesn't…if there's any problem at all, here's my phone number, both at work and at home. Call me anytime."

"I understand. I'm sure we'll be fine. I've had difficult patients before, much worse than your brother." Amanda didn't say it aloud, but the most difficult man she'd had to deal with was not a patient, but a doctor. She smiled at the incredulous look on Rafik's face. "Yes, it's true. It's hard for anyone to be sick and helpless, but for men who are used to being in charge, it's doubly difficult. So I know where he's coming from. I'm sure we'll get along just fine."

She hoped Rafik couldn't read her mind at that point. She hoped he didn't guess that she was far from sure about anything. About whether his brother would cooperate or whether they'd ever get along as patient and nurse, which was all they'd ever be.

"I'll call anyway and give you updated progress reports," Amanda continued. "I appreciate your confidence in me."

He smiled and shook her hand and went off to talk to his wife about plans to drive back to the city. She watched the two of them and wondered how long they'd been married. Their affection for each other and their closeness was obvious from across the room even though Amanda couldn't hear what they were saying. She couldn't help but wish it had been that brother who was the patient. Or would he, too, have become a difficult patient after an accident like that? Was Rahman going to turn into a charming replica of his brother when he got well? If he did, would she live to see it happen? Or by that time, would he have turned her into a mere shadow of her former self, in worse shape emotionally than when she'd arrived? She would not, could not, let that happen.

Chapter Three

Once the family had left, bidding Rahman tearful good-byes, Amanda gave him his medicine and lingered at the side of his bed. He looked exhausted, with dark circles under his eyes, his cheeks almost cavernous. His temperature was normal but his hands were cold. She pulled the down comforter up to his chin.

"How do you feel?" she asked.

"Tired."

"What about something hot to drink?" she asked.

"Too late, Clarice has probably gone to bed," he said, referring to the housekeeper.

"I think I can figure out how to turn on the stove," she said. "Hot chocolate?" she asked.

"If you like," he said.

Amanda decided she would like. She found a tin of cocoa powder, sugar, milk, even marshmallows in the modern kitchen with polished copper pots hanging from the ceiling. Yeast rolls were rising on the granite counter, giving off a wonderful smell. She felt a surprising sense of well-being, of being cared for, though she herself was the caregiver. She couldn't remember the last time anyone had fixed breakfast for her.

Yes, she had a difficult job ahead of her, but where else could she work where she could live in luxury with a housekeeper who made delicious food. She might get spoiled before her stay here was over. Then again, there was the trade-off of caring for one stubborn sheik. Amanda went back to his room with two cups of steaming cocoa on a tray. Rahman's eyes were closed. Oh, no, she wasn't going to let this happen again.

"Rahman," she said softly.

He opened his eyes and looked at her as if he was surprised to see her. She felt a pang of guilt. She vowed not to let him down again. After a long moment he said, "You didn't forget."

"Of course I didn't forget. You're my patient."

"That's all?" he asked, slowly sitting up in bed.

What was she supposed to say to that? She removed her cup then set the tray securely on his bed.

"Isn't that enough?" she asked.

"Of course." He picked up his cup and sipped his cocoa. "It's more than I deserve. A beautiful nurse who can cook, too."

She smiled. "Most women can stir up a little hot chocolate."

"Really? Lisa couldn't."

"Who's Lisa?" she asked.

He gave her a long look with his eyes narrowed almost to slits. "An old friend," he said at last. Then he put his cup down and stared into space. She could have kicked herself. She'd forgotten they weren't going to pry into each other's personal lives. If they started, she didn't know where it would end. There were some things best left unsaid. Certainly he felt the same way if the look on his face was any indication.

"I'll let you get some sleep," she said, taking his tray. He didn't seem to hear her. Or if he did, he had nothing to say. She gave him his medicine and he drank it from a paper cup without complaining, though she knew it had a bitter taste.

She said good-night. He nodded, but he still didn't say anything.

Amanda went to her own room, the charming suite decorated in the blue of the lake and the yellow of the California sun and got into her nightgown. She set her alarm to wake her up at four-hour intervals to give her patient more medication. When her alarm beeped, she threw on her flannel robe, walked down the hall and measured out a spoonful of purple liquid. She sat on the edge of his bed, held his head up with one hand and spooned it into his mouth. He was so groggy he wasn't really awake, but he got the medicine down. That was all that counted.

Then he went back to sleep and so did she. Sort of. She kept the intercom on so she could hear him if he needed her, so she heard every moan and every sigh, every time he tried to turn over on his cracked rib. He must be very uncomfortable. Of course he was.

Amanda herself had never experienced such creature comforts before. Her luxurious suite was down the hall from his with a separate entrance and its own deck. She lay in bed that morning for a few precious minutes, admiring the vaulted ceiling with its exposed natural beams, the planked floor covered by a thick patterned carpet. The huge king-size bed with a down comforter and an adjoining bathroom that was the size of her whole motel room. The sun was peeking over the mountains, the sky an incredible lapis lazuli blue. It was time to get up and see how her patient was doing.

She allowed herself another moment to appreciate the blissfully quiet house. Outside her window a red-headed woodpecker pecked away at the bark of a snow-laden fir tree. The smell of coffee and cinnamon rolls floated from the kitchen. How could anyone complain about having to stay here in one of the country's most scenic vacation spots? How indeed, unless of course, they had no choice about it. To think she was getting paid to do it.

"Amanda?" Rahman's voice came loud and clear over the intercom. "Where are you?"

Instantly she was reminded just why she was getting paid to do it. She jumped up, dressed quickly and walked into Rahman's room smiling cheerfully. A moment later her smile faded. He was sitting up in bed glaring at her.

"Why don't you wear a uniform?" he demanded, his eyes traveling up and down her body, from her turtleneck T-shirt to her thick-stockinged feet hastily thrust into Birkenstock shoes.

"You want me to wear a uniform?" she asked, startled. "Why?"

"Then you'd look more like a nurse."

She wanted to tell him it was none of his business what she wore. If he didn't think she looked like a nurse, that was his problem. "Why don't you wear a long robe and a white headdress around your head?" she asked. "Then you'd look more like a sheik."

"How do you know I don't?" he countered. "When I'm well, that is. I don't usually wear pajamas during the day. But I understand what you're saying. If I were a private duty nurse I suppose I'd dress casually, wear comfortable clothes, sweaters, slacks...but we sheiks have our reputations to think of. Yes, I'll have to get out my ceremonial clothes for you one of these days.''

"I'll look forward to that," she said. "Of course if it's a white uniform and a starched hat and clunky white shoes you want, you're going to love Nurse Whitmore.''

"Who?"

"She's going to be the weekend nurse. She's exactly what you were looking for. Gray hair and fiftyish. I don't know about the thick ankles. You'll have to see for yourself.''

"Why wasn't I consulted about this weekend nurse?"

"The agency is sending her. Your brother set it up with them. I thought he told you.''

"No," he said brusquely. "I don't know why I need a weekend nurse. If you're not here, I can take care of myself. What are you going to do on the weekends anyway?''

"I don't know. I'll think of something. My friend has invited me to stay at her house. But just for two days. I'll be back Sunday evening. You'll hardly know I'm gone. A five-day work week is pretty normal, even for nurses. Everybody needs a break. You wouldn't want me to be subjected to burnout, would you?''

She didn't like the look of disapproval on his face so she changed the subject.

"Turn over," she said, her tone just as brusque as his. Amanda refused to let him make her feel guilty about taking days off. If she didn't, she wouldn't be able to do her job. Even with the days off, she wasn't sure.

She ripped the wrapper off a disposable syringe and he winced in advance. "Are you going to do what I think you're going to do?" he asked.

"Give you a shot in the butt," she said. She refused to baby him. He didn't need it and he didn't want it.

He turned over and she pulled his pajama bottoms down. At the sight of his attractive backside, her hand shook. Luckily he was facedown and he couldn't tell. She inserted the needle, pushed the medicine in and pulled it out.

He turned over. "You're good," he said with a grin that covered whatever pain he felt. "I hardly felt a thing."

Before she could reply to this flattering assessment of her injection technique, the housekeeper knocked on the door with his breakfast tray. Amanda's mouth watered at the sight of the half grapefruit, bacon, hot rolls and coffee. She'd sat down to dinner with the family last night for a wonderful dinner of lasagna and Caesar salad but Rahman had been conspicuously absent. Everyone had been aware of his absence, thinking of him sitting alone in his room brooding. That had cast a pall over the dinner table. They spoke of trivial matters in hushed voices. Amanda didn't realize how hungry she was this morning until she saw his attractive breakfast tray.

"Where's Amanda's?" Rahman asked Clarice.

"In the dining room," Clarice replied, setting his tray in front of him on his bed. "I didn't realize she'd want to eat in here."

"I want her to eat in here. I hate eating alone. Food as good as yours deserves to be shared, Clarice," he added as an afterthought.

"Don't try that flattery on me, Rahman," the woman said, her hands on her broad hips. "I know you too well. You haven't changed a smidge since you were a boy."

"Why do I get the feeling that's not a compliment?" Rahman said when she left the room.

"She's been with the family for a long time, I gather."

"She and her husband Andre came with my parents when they immigrated to the U.S. Andre's in the city taking care of some things for my parents just now. The original plan was for them to manage the house in the city, but they weren't comfortable there. Too much noise, too many cars. They like it here and we like having them. Yes, I'm afraid she knows me too well and she isn't above putting me in my place."

He pointed to the chair next to the bed. "Sit down," he commanded. "She'll be right back with your food. I guarantee you'll put on at least ten pounds before you leave here. It looks to me like you could use them." Again he gave her an appraising look.

Amanda didn't know if that was a compliment or not. In any case, she sat down. Sure enough, Clarice came back with a tray for her too.

"Sure you want to eat here with him?" she asked Amanda with a sideways glance at Rahman. "Don't you let the boy push you around any. If he gives you any trouble, you give me a shout."

"Thank you," Amanda said. "I'll do that."

"Wait a minute. I've been outnumbered," Rahman grumbled, but he picked up his spoon and began to eat.

Amanda agreed. This food was too good not to be shared. Not that they talked during breakfast. They simply ate in a companionable silence. She was pleased to see how much Rahman ate.

She smiled her approval at the sight of his clean plate. "You'll need all the energy you can get," she said.

"For what?" he asked. "For lying in bed all day?"

"Oh, no. That's over with. If you want to get back to normal you're going to have to work at it. The physical therapist is coming today to teach us both what you're

supposed to do. Then we can continue to do the daily
exercises and she'll come once a week.''

"Once a week? How many weeks do you think I'll
be here?''

"I don't know. That depends on you.''

"Let's get started," he said.

Amanda nodded. This was a good sign. He wanted to
get well, and he was willing to work at it. She couldn't
ask for more.

But that was before the therapist arrived. When she
did, and they wheeled him into the game room that used
to have a pool table in the middle but was now the exercise room, he looked around at the traction tables, the
training stairs, the mats and the pulleys and the balance
boards, and he turned to Amanda.

"Whoa," he said. "What's all this?''

Amanda deferred to the therapist, a sturdy young
blond woman named Heidi who looked strong enough
physically and mentally to handle Rahman on her own.
She explained to Rahman and Amanda what he was supposed to do every day. She helped Rahman up and put
him through the paces. Just a small workout, but obviously much more than he'd anticipated. Not that he complained or even moaned when Heidi pushed him farther
along the parallel bars than he wanted to go, but Amanda
saw his mouth tighten and his jaw clench.

Amanda stayed right behind the therapist, following
her instructions, helping her, taking notes, knowing that
the more she could absorb, the faster, the less she'd have
to depend on Heidi.

Rahman was breathing hard when he finally collapsed
in his wheelchair. Amanda checked his pulse. It was fast
but not outside the normal range. He gave her an in-
scrutable look before she took her hand away. Was he

remembering the time in the hospital when he grabbed her wrist and didn't let go? She was. The memory brought the color to her cheeks. She had to turn away and feign interest in something besides her patient. Rahman wheeled himself back to his room and Amanda went to the door with the therapist.

"Nice place they've got here," Heidi commented, with a glance at the view of the lake from the huge living room window. "He's very lucky. Most patients have to come in to the clinic for their therapy. And they don't have a private nurse."

"Don't let him hear you say that about being lucky," Amanda cautioned. "He feels anything but. He's got a cracked rib, a tube in his chest...but you know all that."

"I also know he's got the best that money can buy."

"He still has a long way to go." No amount of money could buy his health back. Yes, it helped to have the facilities at hand. But if Rahman didn't take advantage of them, didn't work at it, he might as well be in the county hospital, sharing a ward with four other men and ringing a bell to summon an overworked nurse who had too little time and too many patients to give him the personal care he was used to.

Did he appreciate what his family and his money were doing for him? Amanda didn't know. She thought it likely he took it all for granted. After all, wealth and luxury were all he'd ever known.

After the therapist left, Amanda went back to Rahman's room.

"Want to take a shower?" she asked, helping him shift his body back into bed.

"No," he said. "I didn't do much, but I'm bushed."

"Then I'll give you a sponge bath in bed."

"What?" His eyes widened in alarm. "No, you won't."

Rahman could just imagine her taking his clothes off, rubbing his naked body with a wet sponge. He had a strong, unwanted reaction to her just holding his wrist and taking his pulse. His heart had sped up, he felt like his skin was on fire. Of course that could be because of the unaccustomed exercise. But the thought of her bathing him made it happen all over, that rush of excitement, a jolt of adrenaline. He couldn't let her know the effect she had on him. He had to act cool.

"No thanks, Nurse Reston. I'll take the shower. If you insist."

"I just thought…" she began.

"I know what you thought. You thought I couldn't do it myself. I know I look like a weakling. How do you think I feel? I could hardly get up those training stairs. Me. The guy who used to spend the day up here skiing, then head back to the city and have a game of racquetball at the club before dinner. I think I can take a shower by myself." If only she'd known him before. She must think he was a wimp, a coward. He hated that. It made him react more strongly than he should.

"Fine," she said. "I don't want to do anything for you that you can do for yourself. The goal is to get you back to your former life."

"That's my goal," he said. "What's yours?"

"The same."

"I understand. So you can get rid of me and get back to your former life. What was that, Nurse Reston? You know about mine, now tell me what your former life was like." He leaned back against the pillows of his adjustable hospital bed and looked at her with curiosity.

Amanda hesitated. Rahman was afraid for a moment

that she was going to tell him it was none of his business, but she didn't. She perched on the arm of a large, overstuffed chair.

"I worked in a big-city hospital in the trauma center. I saw people like you come in every day. Only their injuries usually weren't from ski accidents. They were more likely car accidents or motorcycles, gunshot wounds or heart attacks."

"Sounds exciting," he said. "Is that why you liked it?"

"Yes. You patch people up and then they go into surgery or long-term care or something. But you don't follow up on them. You have no time because there are always more people rushed in in ambulances, waiting for you. You're never bored."

"Like you are here."

"I didn't say I was bored."

"I'll say it for you. You're bored. Admit it. I'm bored, too. I'd rather be out there." He waved toward the mountain. "So why did you leave?"

"Maybe I was tired of the pressure. Maybe I was ready to be bored."

"You don't follow up on patients, so I assume you don't get attached to them either," he said thoughtfully.

"That's right. Now, about that shower..."

"What were you afraid of?" he asked.

"I wasn't afraid," she protested. "Well, maybe I was afraid I'd feel too bad if they...if they didn't get well."

He nodded slowly. "I can imagine," he said softly. "So that way, you avoided the pain of losing a patient."

"I see you have me all analyzed," she said lightly.

Rahman shifted in bed. His ribs hurt, but he wanted to hear more. No, he didn't have her analyzed. But he was trying. "Why did you decide to be a nurse?" he asked.

She looked at him for a long moment. Was she wondering if she should go on or stop right there? Was she sorry she'd already said too much?

"My mother was sick a lot when I was young. I took care of her, if a kid can really take care of a parent. I did my best." She hesitated and blinked hard as though to keep back tears.

Rahman drew his brows together. Now he wished he hadn't asked. He'd brought back painful memories. He hated to see her cry. She was so strong, so sure of herself. He thought of her as someone who could face emergencies and never break down. Or had she?

"I can't imagine myself taking care of my parents, not that young," he said. "You must have been quite a girl."

She shook off his compliment with a slight shrug of her shoulders. "You do what you have to do. I was an only child. My dad went to work every day."

"I'm sorry I brought up painful memories," he said. "I didn't mean to." He leaned forward. He wanted to hold her hand. To put his arms around her and comfort her. But he was stuck in this bed, unable to help himself, let alone anyone else. Maybe she wouldn't want his comfort anyway.

"It's all right," she said, taking a shaky breath. "She died before I started high school. After that I took care of the house and my dad as best I could. So when it came time to decide what I wanted to do, he suggested nursing. He thought I'd be good at it."

"He was right," Rahman said. No wonder she'd chosen to work in trauma. Of course she didn't want to see any patients die. It would bring back painful memories.

She didn't say any more. She stood up and went to
the side of his bed. He knew what was next. Story time
was over. So he gave up and let her help him hobble
into the shower. After she turned on the shower and
adjusted the water temperature and closed the bathroom
door he got undressed, slowly and painfully, and sat on
a stool under the spray of water.

When he came out wrapped in a terry-cloth robe, she
was waiting for him with clean pajamas. Tactfully she
left the room while he dressed. Rahman knew it would
be easier if she helped him, but he was not going to let
her see him naked and he was going to do as much as
he could for himself. No matter how much harder it was.

They had lunch together in his room. She didn't say
much, neither did he. Rahman wanted to know more
about her, but he was afraid he'd pushed her as far as
she would go. Clarice had brought them big bowls of
vegetable soup with homemade bread. He ate half of his
then leaned back against his pillows. Amanda gave him
more medicine and then he couldn't hold his eyes open
any longer. A nap. He was taking a nap, he thought as
he drifted off to sleep. Like a damned baby. Before he
fell asleep, the image of Amanda's face floated across
Rahman's mind. She looked sad and he wanted to cheer
her up, but he was tired, so tired.

Amanda was ready for a nap, too. She watched en-
viously as Rahman closed his eyes and slept. The long
night of interrupted sleep and the morning with the physical therapist had tired her, too. She stood at the side of
his bed thinking how vulnerable he looked when he was
asleep. Not at all the bored, rebellious patient who hated
being helpless and at her mercy. She had seen it in his
eyes, his stubbornness. He needed her help in the shower
and getting dressed, but he'd never ask for it. Not that

she had any desire to see him without his clothes. It was bad enough she could imagine his broad shoulders, tapered waist, chest with a sprinkling of dark hair... She turned abruptly and left the room. Her mouth was so dry she went to get herself a glass of water and give herself a stern talking to about being attracted to a patient.

Amanda headed for her suite, but she didn't get a chance to sleep. Rosie called and came by with the twins to see how she was doing. And, as she confessed, "to see that house." They tiptoed in, so as not to wake the patient, and Rosie was suitably impressed with the view, the comfortable, expensive but unpretentious furnishings and best of all, Amanda's suite.

"This is gorgeous," Rosie said, looking around at the oak dresser and pale yellow walls and the walk-in closet. "I had no idea you'd get the royal treatment."

"And the food. Rosie, you have to meet the housekeeper."

Amanda took her friend and the twins to the kitchen where Clarice was stirring a sauce for the chicken she was making for dinner. The smell of wine and garlic wafted from the pot on the stove. Clarice had just taken a batch of chocolate chip cookies out of the oven and the twins were wide-eyed with delight when the housekeeper seated them at the kitchen table and served them cookies and milk.

"It's good to have children in the house again," Clarice said to Amanda after she'd been introduced to Rosie and her girls. "We've got Rafik married off so I have my fingers crossed for them to produce a baby or two, but what to do about Rahman?" she asked, her forehead furrowed with worry lines.

"Well, I'm sure once he's well..." Amanda said.

"He must be quite a catch," Rosie commented. "He's rich and I understand quite handsome."

Clarice nodded. "Some people think he's arrogant, but that's just a pose, to protect himself from getting hurt. Not many people realize that, and he wouldn't admit it for the world, but I've known him all his life. He doesn't want people to know how much he cares. Sometimes I think he cares too much, as he did for...never mind. I'm speaking out of turn."

Amanda wondered if she was going to say "Lisa." The mysterious Lisa. If she was more than just "a friend" and he cared so much about her, where was she now when he needed her? Before Amanda could pursue the subject, Rosie told her she had to get back to work. She was swamped with job openings so as soon as Amanda was finished with this job, she had other patients who were looking for a home nurse. Before she left, she wanted to see the rehab setup, so they left the twins dunking the cookies in their milk and walked down the hall to the ballroom.

Rahman woke up from a dream in which a nurse in a starched white uniform was giving him a shower. She looked like Amanda with her dark hair and blue eyes, but it couldn't be Amanda. Amanda was a professional who was only doing her job and he would never let her wash him. This shower had overtones of being not only for hygienic purposes, but personally stimulating as well. The memory lingered, the feeling that her hands had been all over him made his body react in a way that was reassuring as well as disturbing.

He took a sip of water from the glass on his bedside table and looked out the window as the late afternoon sun touched the crest of the mountains. It wasn't surprising he'd dream about Amanda. She was the only woman around and she was attractive. That was precisely why he hadn't wanted her around. Stirring up feelings he couldn't control. Nurse dreams were common even among men who were healthy. So why worry? It was just a dream.

He heard a small sound like the whisper of a breeze and swiveled his head in the direction of the door to his room. He blinked. There in the doorway stood two small girls who were staring at him. They looked exactly alike from their short brown hair to their striped overalls, pink shirts and small white sturdy shoes.

He must be hallucinating again. It was one thing to hallucinate a nurse or a doctor, but little girls?

"Hello?" he said in a voice as rough as gravel. "Are you real?"

They burst into giggles. "'Course we're real," one said. "I'm Sara and she's Nora."

"Come in here so I can see you. You look exactly alike," he said, not really believing his eyes.

"Cuz we're twins," Nora explained as they stepped through the doorway.

"Me, too, I'm a twin," he said, pushing himself up to a sitting position.

They stared at him in disbelief. Maybe they'd never seen grown-up twins. "Where's the other one?" Sara demanded.

"The other twin? He doesn't live here. He's gone home."

"Don't you miss him?" Nora asked.

Rahman nodded. He missed Rafik badly. If Rafik were here he'd never let Rahman wallow in self-pity. He'd yell at him, make fun of him, whatever it took to shake him out of his doldrums. As children, they had been as close as twins could be. They'd vowed to never live apart. To take the world by storm, to never let anyone or anything come between them. So much for childish plans.

"Where did you girls come from?" he asked. "Is there some kind of twin convention going on?"

"What's that?" Nora asked.

"Never mind."

"We better go," Sara whispered to her sister. "We're not 'sposed to wake up the patient. He's sick and he's kind of cranky."

"Maybe you'd be cranky, too, if you had to stay in bed all day," Rahman said with a half smile.

They both nodded sympathetically. What could be worse for a kid than to be told she had to stay in bed all day?

"Before you go, tell me where you came from," Rahman asked. "How did you get here?"

"Our mom brought us. She's Amanda's friend. Amanda is the best nurse there is. That's what my mom says," Nora said.

"Your mom is right," Rahman agreed. He didn't want them to go. He hadn't thought about his ankle or his chest since they had appeared. He didn't know any children. He hadn't known they could be good company. He thought they'd just be a lot of trouble. He had no idea they'd be so cute. "Do you ever play tricks on people, like telling them you're the other twin?"

They broke into grins, showing gaps in their baby teeth and nodded. "Hey," he said, "would you like to see a picture of me and my brother when we were about your age?"

"Okay."

''Bring me that big leather book there on the desk,'' he directed.

Nora brought the book and she and her sister stood next to his bed while he opened the scrapbook his mother had brought to cheer him up. Little did she know it had done just the opposite which was why he hadn't looked at it since she had left. Rahman hated seeing pictures of himself doing the things he couldn't do now. He made him wonder if he'd ever do them again or how long it would take before he was even half as healthy as he'd been. But if he didn't go beyond the first few pages of his childhood, he ought to be able to look at it without getting depressed. He wanted to entertain these little girls, to at least keep them around for a few more minutes before someone realized they were missing and were disturbing the ''cranky'' patient.

''Okay,'' he said, turning the pages. ''Here's my brother and me at our school with our class.''

''But they're all boys,'' Sara said.

''Yes, that's the way it is in my country. The girls go to one school, the boys go to another.''

''That's funny.''

Yes, it did seem funny after all these years in the States. He and Rafik had been sent to boarding school here then college. Now he was completely Americanized. At least, he thought he was.

As he turned the pages, Nora and Sara pointed their little fingers at the pictures, asking who was who and where they were. They stared at a family photo that had been taken by a professional photographer when he was eight or so and they looked at him and back at the photo for a long time.

''You look different,'' they said.

"When you're my age, you'll probably look different, too," he said.

"How old are you?" Nora asked.

He was about to tell her, when Amanda and another woman, presumably their mother came to the door.

"Girls," their mother scolded, "what are you doing in here? I told you not to…"

"Disturb the cranky patient," Rahman said. "It's all right. They're not disturbing me."

"Rahman," Amanda said, "this is my friend Rosie. She runs a staffing agency. She's the one who got me this job."

"Then I have her to thank for bringing you to me," he said. "I feel very fortunate," he said to Rosie.

"Yes, you are," Rosie said. "She's in great demand."

"Mom," Nora said. "He's a twin, too."

"Really?"

"Yes, look, here's their picture." She picked up the book from where it was lying open on Rahman's lap.

"Wait a minute," Rosie cautioned. "I don't think you ought to…"

"It's okay," Rahman said.

Rosie glanced at the picture and commented on the unusual life of twins. Then she gathered her daughters, apologized for the interruption, said goodbye and suddenly they were gone, all of them, Amanda, too. The room was quiet, too quiet. He put his hand on the buzzer and hit it a few times. Damn it, where was she?

"Sorry," Amanda said breathlessly when she came into his room. "I hope the girls didn't wake you. We'd left them having cookies in the kitchen with Clarice. I should have known things were too quiet."

"Cookies? Why can't I have cookies?" he demanded.

"Of course you can. I'll get them."

She came back with a tray of cookies and two glasses of milk.

He frowned. "I'd rather have a beer."

"Sorry, it wouldn't react well with the medication. Besides I don't think it goes well with cookies."

"You win." He reached for a cookie.

She sat across the room with a glass of milk and nibbled on a cookie.

"Twins run in families, don't they?" he said.

"Yes, I think so."

"I wouldn't mind having children like that," he said thoughtfully. "Funny, I never thought about having kids. I really never imagined getting married at all. When we were ten years old, Rafik and I promised each other we wouldn't. Then Rafik...but that's another story."

It was true, he had never thought of marrying Lisa, or anybody else. Even after Rafik got married and he felt jealous and left out, he was not ready to get married. But now, seeing those girls...he felt a little differently. They were so cute with their missing teeth, their girlish giggles, he could almost imagine... What would it feel like to bring babies into the world? To watch them grow up, to be responsible for their education, their morals, their future? No, he wasn't ready for that kind of responsibility. He couldn't even get himself down the ski slope without hurting himself. First he had to find somebody who'd marry him. Easier said than done.

"Yes, they're awfully cute," Amanda said with a wistful note in her voice.

"What about you?" he asked. "Do you want kids?"

"Oh, I don't know. Maybe someday. It's hard to imagine without..." The wistfulness was gone. She sounded deliberately casual.

"Without someone to marry," he said, nodding in agreement. "What do you mean, 'someday'? How old are you?"

"Thirty-one," she said.

"I thought you'd tell me it was none of my business," he said.

She shook her head, then went to his bed and removed his tray. "My age isn't a secret.

"What is?" he asked. She had secrets, he knew she did.

Ignoring his question, she picked up the scrapbook from the side of his bed. "Was this what you were showing them?" she asked.

"My mother brought my scrapbook for me. She thought it would cheer me up. But I haven't felt like looking at it until those little girls came in. I wanted them to see pictures of me and Rafik when we were kids."

"Can I look at it?" she asked.

"If you want to." The truth was he didn't want her to see it. He didn't want her to look into his life the way it used to be. It made him feel more vulnerable than he already was. But he didn't want to appear to be rude, either.

She sat on the stool at the edge of his bed with the scrapbook in her lap. "Where was this taken?" she asked, pausing to look at a photo of a family posed in front of a villa on the sea.

"That's the family compound on the Arabian Gulf."

"That's where you grew up?" Amanda asked. She was stunned by the beauty of the place, by the white buildings, the profusion of flowers and the blue water in the distance.

"Yes. I haven't been back for years. But it was a great

place to grow up. Rafik and I learned to sail and swim there. We had acres of land to run wild when we could escape from our tutor.''

''You had each other, so you were never lonely,'' she said. Again that wistful note in her voice.

''That's right. Plus various cousins who came to visit. But now...''

''Now your brother is married. Do you miss him?'' she asked. She hadn't realized how close twins could be. Seeing Rosie's girls and hearing about Rahman and his brother, she was beginning to realize what a gap in your life it could be to grow up and be separated from your closest friend. Closer than regular siblings, closer than any friend.

''Miss Rafik? No,'' he said. ''He's married.''

''Well, I'm envious. I was an only child. I would have loved to have a brother or sister. I can't imagine how it would be to be a twin. If I did have kids, I'd like to have several, so they wouldn't be lonely the way I was.''

''Any prospects?'' he asked lightly.

She stood up and went to the window to draw the shade.

''Sorry,'' he said contritely. ''None of my business. I just don't understand how somebody who looks like you, who's as competent as you are, isn't married. What's wrong with those men in Chicago?''

She almost blurted out the answer: *They're married.* But she caught herself in time. She had no reason to confide in him her disastrous mistake of trusting someone she shouldn't have trusted. She turned to look at him. There was a shadow across his face hiding his expression. She hoped he'd gotten the message. She was not going to talk about her personal life any more than she'd already done. Especially when the subject was her nonexistent love life. She'd already said too much about her past.

"Oh, well," he said. "Their loss is my gain."

"You're in a philosophical mood," she said with a smile. And what a relief it was. Was this what he used to be like before the accident? Was this what he'd be like when he recovered? It was an intriguing thought. One that cheered her up. Made her job all worthwhile.

"Why not?" he said.

She went back to his bedside, sat down next to him and picked up his scrapbook.

"Anything else I should see?" she asked, happy to switch the subject from her past to his.

"Just the story of my life. Not that interesting. Unless you find me fascinating." He grinned at her and she felt a little tingle run up her spine. He was a flirt. She shouldn't be surprised. That was what she'd expected when she first met him, but she hadn't seen that side of him until now.

"Doesn't everyone?" she teased, thumbing through his book.

He reached for her hand and she stopped turning the pages. He wrapped his fingers around hers and the atmosphere changed from lighthearted banter to something else. She didn't know what to call it. She only knew she was acutely aware of the strength and warmth of his grip. She tried to say something, something that would break the tension, but she couldn't speak around the lump that was stuck in her throat.

"No," he said at last in a deep, quiet voice. "Not everyone." His face was so close to hers she felt his warm breath on her cheek. Her heart was pounding so loud she was afraid he could hear it. She glanced down at a photo of him on a beach, surrounded by a crowd of

young women, all smiling, all looking like they were
having a good time. All looking like they found the sheik
extremely fascinating, no matter what he said to the con-
trary. Amanda felt a pang of jealousy for these lovely
women. How ridiculous that was, to be jealous of his
girlfriends, of whom he obviously had many. She was
not in their league and never would be.

Amanda pulled her hand away. "What about her?"
she asked, pointing to an attractive blonde in a bikini.

He leaned over Amanda's shoulder. She felt a shiver
go up her spine. What on earth was wrong with her? She
bit her lip. This was a terrible idea letting a patient affect
her this way. She shouldn't have any trouble separating
her personal life from her professional life. She never
had before until... No, she couldn't let it happen again.
Hadn't she gotten a lesson back in Chicago she'd never
forget? Of course the man was attractive. Of course he
knew it and so did all these women in the photo, from
the way they were looking at him. He was the last person
she should be attracted to.

"Her?" he said, obviously oblivious to the effect he
was having on Amanda. "Let me see. Where was that
taken? I know, Laguna Beach. I don't think I remember
her name."

"What about her or her or her?" she asked, pointing
to the others.

He shrugged. "No."

"No wonder you haven't gotten married yet. First you
have to remember their names."

"Oh," he said. "Is that it? I wondered what I'd been
doing wrong."

She shook her head and closed the book. "You've
had quite a past, Rahman."

"Maybe so, but as you see, it's an open book," he

said. "Which is more than I can say about yours. When am I going to find out what's in your past?"

"That wasn't part of the bargain," she said, closing his scrapbook and standing up. She left the room quickly hoping and praying he couldn't tell her knees were wobbling. Or guess why he'd affected her that way.

Chapter Four

Amanda had had no intention of allowing herself to be tricked into confiding in Rahman. But she had to admit she enjoyed their sparring and she thought he did, too. But the next day, by some unspoken agreement, it was back to business. She didn't tease him about his girl-friends or even cast a glance at his scrapbook. He didn't joke with her or ask any impertinent questions. They were back to being a nurse and a patient. It was a relief to her. If it was a disappointment, too, but she wasn't ready to admit it, even to herself.

She decided that he, too, was having second thoughts about their getting too close. The schedule was the same. Breakfast in his room. Physical therapy in the ballroom and then lunch, then a nap. But without the camaraderie of the day before. They carefully avoided talking about their personal lives, either the past or the future.

Clarice asked Amanda if Rahman was up to having dinner in the dining room.

''I don't like to see the room going to waste,'' Clarice

told Amanda as she put a small roast in the oven. "Too bad for you to have to eat with him in his sick room. Couldn't we push him up to the table in his wheelchair?"

When Amanda mentioned the idea, Rahman agreed, but when she went to get him for dinner, he was back to looking at his scrapbook and looking morose.

"What's wrong?" she asked.

"Nothing." He slammed the book shut. "I wish my family hadn't brought this book. There are too many memories in here. It's hard enough—" He bit off his words and didn't finish his sentence.

"You're going to get better, you know. You're going to recover completely, according to the doctor. Your life will go on just as it always did. Friends, activities, fun, sports. One of these days you'll be sailing again, skiing again—"

"With who?" he demanded, cutting her off.

"You must have a lot of friends," she said, helping him into his wheelchair. "I heard they all came to see you in the hospital."

"The ones who are still alive, yes," he said bitterly.

She was so startled she stopped pushing him toward the dining room.

"I...I don't know what to say. Did someone die?" she asked. Then she could have kicked herself for prying.

"Yes, she did. She's dead. You won't see any pictures of her in here because I took them all out. She was the most vibrant, exciting person I've ever known. And she's gone. What's the point of it all?" he asked.

Amanda didn't know the answer to that. And even if she did, she didn't think he wanted to hear it. When they got to the table and she'd taken a seat across from him in his wheelchair, she noticed he was staring off into space, his face frozen in a mask of despair.

"Maybe this wasn't such a good idea after all," she said from the other side of the oval, polished wood table.

"It's fine," he said, bringing his gaze back to her and stabbing a piece of lettuce with his fork. "No reason you should have to eat in the room with the me."

"I really don't mind. It was Clarice's idea we eat out here."

"Yeah, I know. She thinks I'm malingering."

"No, she doesn't. She's never said that to me," Amanda said.

"She doesn't have to say anything. It's the way she looks at me. The same disapproving way she used to look at me when I was young and she knew I was hiding something or doing something I wasn't supposed to. She's not good at hiding her disappointment. I think I was more afraid of not living up to her standards than even my father's. That's strange, isn't it?"

"I think she might have that effect on anybody. But this time, I think she merely thought it would make a change and it would cheer you up. If it doesn't…"

"What am I supposed to do to show how cheerful I am? Tell jokes? Laugh?" he asked. He gave a loud, fake laugh that startled her.

"Look, Rahman…" She didn't finish her sentence because Clarice came through the door with a large baking dish of scalloped potatoes in cheese sauce.

"Now what?" the housekeeper said, setting the dish on the table and pausing to frown at Rahman. "What was all that noise out here? Seems to me some people around here have forgotten their hospitality. Miss Amanda here is a guest in this house and in the absence of your parents, Rahman, you are the host. I heard you talking all the way from the kitchen, in a way unbecoming of the master of the house. Yes, I did. I know you were brought up better than that. Sick or well, you have an obligation to your guest to be polite. I wouldn't blame her for picking up and leaving for a better job. You're not the only patient on this mountain.''

Rahman's face turned a dull red. Amanda felt for him. On the other hand, she wished she could talk to him the way the housekeeper did. Sick or not, mourning a lost love or not, sometimes he did act like a spoiled child.

''I apologize,'' he said to Amanda through stiff lips. ''I have forgotten. My parents would be disappointed to say the least, if they'd seen me just then and heard what I said.''

''I understand that when you're in pain and you're suffering from a loss, you're not yourself,'' Amanda said. ''I'm sure they'd understand, too.''

''I'm not sure of that,'' he said with a look at Clarice who was still standing in the dining room door with her hands on her hips. ''They would say there was no excuse. Believe it or not, I was raised with better manners. From now on, I'll try to control myself. I don't want to lose you,'' he added in a low voice.

Amanda nodded. She didn't know what to say. The concern in his voice was sincere and his apology sounded heartfelt. He didn't know it, but it would take more than an outburst of temper from a sick patient to get her to leave.

When Clarice had gone back to the kitchen, Rahman looked up from his plate. His forehead was furrowed in a frown. ''You wouldn't leave, would you?'' he asked Amanda.

''Not as long as Clarice is here making food like this,'' she said, spooning some potatoes onto her plate.

He breathed a sigh of relief. "Thank God for Clarice," he said. He paused and took a deep breath. "Tell me, Amanda, what are you going to do on your weekend off?" he asked pleasantly.

She blinked in surprise. He'd certainly made a quick switch from the crabby, sarcastic patient to the genial host. Just what Clarice and his family would want him to be. He didn't even seem angry or resentful any more of her taking her days off.

"Well," she said. "I don't know. Since I don't know the area and I don't ski..."

"Maybe I can make some suggestions," he said with a smile.

"You should do that more often," she said.

"What, make suggestions?" he asked.

"No, smile."

He nodded in recognition of the same remark he'd made to her, and smiled again, this time with genuine amusement. "You could take a cable car or a tram up above the lake for a great view. There's one at Squaw Valley and another at Heavenly."

"That sounds like a good idea. Do you know who Mark Twain is?" she asked.

"The one who said the coldest winter I ever spent was a summer in San Francisco?"

"Yes, that's the one," she said with a smile, trying to hide her surprise that not only did he know who the American author was, he could also quote him. "Well, he also said that Lake Tahoe was 'surely the fairest sight on the whole Earth,' or something like that. So I want to see it from every angle."

"You'll need a car. Do you have one?" he asked.

"No, I sold my car before I came out here. I rented

one for a few days, but I really need to buy one. I just haven't had a chance to go out looking.''

"Use mine," he said.

"Oh, I couldn't do that."

"Why not? It's just sitting in the garage. You'll need it to get around. I'll draw you a map of where you should go."

"Thank you. I appreciate that," she said. Was this the same man who'd objected so strongly to her taking a day off, who was now telling her where to go and how to get there? Talk about Dr. Jekyll and Mr. Hyde.

After dinner, he was still in a good mood. Of course that could have something to do with Clarice's delicious apple pie she'd served for dessert. She served it with a smile, too, when she noted the change in Rahman's mood. She suggested they have coffee in the living room where she'd lit a fire in the stone fireplace and then had dimmed the lights.

Through the huge picture windows they could see the tops of the mountains against a dark starry sky.

"This is really beautiful," Amanda said sipping her coffee. "Sometimes I feel like I'm on vacation here."

"Come on," he said. "Even after all that hard work on the parallel bars today?"

"Even after that," she said.

"So, you think you might stay here in California?"

She shrugged lightly. "I don't know. I suspect it will be a little different when I start looking for a full-time job and an apartment and all that."

"You don't have to stay here at the Lake do you?"

"No, but that's where Rosie is, my friend that you met."

"With the twins."

"Yes."

"Have you been to San Francisco?"

"No, I haven't. But there's a nursing conference there next month. Rosie and I are both going. It will give me a chance to see it."

"You might decide it's the right place for you. Tahoe is great for a vacation, but life up here can be rather limited. In the city you have more opportunities. But you know that, coming from a big city."

"Yes, but since I don't know anyone there…"

"You know me," he said.

She glanced at him. His face was half in shadow, half in light from the small table lamp. What did he mean by that? Surely he couldn't imagine her being a part of his social life? She didn't usually hang out with sheiks. She'd seen the photos, she'd heard about his friends. It was a far cry from any life she'd ever known.

"I won't always be an invalid, as you so rightly pointed out. I won't always be so boring."

"Boring. Did I say you were boring?" she asked, startled.

"What did you say?" he asked.

"I may have commented that your behavior was unbecoming."

"I think you said obnoxious."

"That's still not boring," she said.

She couldn't tell, but she thought he might be smiling. She hoped so. He seemed to remember every insult she'd ever directed at him.

"Anyway," he said. "I hope you'll get in touch with me while you're there. I'd like to show you around."

"That would be nice," she said politely, knowing that he was probably just making conversation. When he returned to his old life, he'd have no time for a former nurse. "I've seen pictures and I've heard about how beautiful it is. The ocean, the bay, the cable cars…"

"The bars and the clubs…"

"I'm not much of a night-clubber," she said. She was sure that he was everything she wasn't. A night-clubber, a socialite, a world-traveler, a sophisticate.

"Well then, there's the cracked crab at Fisherman's Wharf, the view from the top of the Mark." As he said the words Rahman could imagine taking Amanda around town to show her the sights. He could picture her face lighting up at the spectacular views, browsing in Chinatown, poking around the back alleys, visiting the fortune cookie factory…yes, he'd like to be there when she saw it all for the first time. He wanted to be the one who showed her his city.

But maybe she'd rather see it with someone else. She'd been so reticent about her personal life. Maybe there was someone back in Chicago. Maybe he'd be joining her here. Whoever he was, Rahman envied him. A woman like Amanda, with her quiet charm and warm sympathy, was not easy to find. Surely someone had claimed her by now. Maybe she was counting the days until he got well and she could get on with her life with the man in her life. The thought of her sightseeing with some other man caused a pain in his chest that had nothing to do with his injuries.

"I wouldn't want you to see it alone," he said pointedly. "That would be a mistake."

"No," she said. "I definitely won't be alone."

He gave her a quick inquisitive glance. He had no idea what she meant by that, but he imagined the worst. She had someone else in mind. That was all she said. That was all she needed to say to have him conjuring up thoughts of her meeting him, whoever he was, at the airport, greeting him warmly. A kiss? A hug? Her face wreathed in smiles. His face was fixed in a frown at the very idea.

He could hint and ask and give her every opportunity, but she clammed up every time he tried to find out for certain if there was a man her life. It was none of his business. Still, wasn't it natural to be curious about someone you were spending so much time with? That was all it was, natural curiosity.

They sat in silence for a long time, each lost in their thoughts. If he hoped she'd finally come through and tell him something, he was disappointed. But just sitting there with her in the semidarkness, watching the flames dance in the company of a woman who radiated good humor and serenity wasn't a bad way to spend an evening. There was something hypnotic about a fire in a fireplace. The pain that had nothing to do with the accident, and had everything to do with the loss of Lisa, had at least temporarily receded. Why, he didn't know.

Two weeks ago he would have been bored silly spending an evening like this. Staying home by the fire was his idea of nothing to do. Not when there were bars and clubs to go to. People to see, to laugh with, to share the good times. He'd always craved action. So had Rafik until he got married. Just as soon as he recovered, Rahman was sure he'd be back out on the party scene. That was the only way to get over Lisa. To fill his life with sound and movement and people. But until then, he would make do with what he had. A nurse who looked like an angel and who knew how to put him in his place. A rare combination. Someone worth staying home for. For now.

On Saturday when the weekend nurse arrived and Amanda got ready to take off, his mood was considerably darker. He knew she was going, but it didn't hit home until he saw Nurse Whitmore arrive with a small overnight bag. He realized with a jolt that Amanda wouldn't be back until Sunday night. He knew she deserved the time off. He knew she needed a break. But that didn't make it any easier to say goodbye to her or to see her dressed in soft dark green wool pants with a matching jacket and plaid scarf, her eyes shining with what he assumed was the anticipation of spending a weekend away from him.

Rahman gritted his teeth to keep from complaining about the arrangement. While she was off to have fun, the weekend stretched ahead of him like a long, dark tunnel and for the life of him he couldn't see the light at the end of it. But he kept his tongue, something he wasn't used to doing and tried to hide his disappointment when she came in to say goodbye.

"Have a great time," he said forcing a smile in attempt to appear cheerful.

She stood at his bedside, her overnight bag on the floor next to her, looking concerned. "I'll leave my number where I can be reached just in case..."

"Just in case? Just in case what? Don't worry about me. I'll be fine. Nurse Whitmore looks to be more than capable." Actually she looked so ferocious he had the feeling she might eat nails for breakfast. "And she's just the type I wished for." Which was true. She was middle-aged, with iron-gray hair, a starchy white uniform, thick-soled shoes and a no-nonsense manner. What if he'd gotten his way? What if he'd gotten her instead of Amanda? He shuddered at the thought.

"That's right," Amanda said with a smile. "I hope I'm not in danger of losing my job to her."

He grinned at the absurdity of the idea and they shared

a moment of good humor there in his room with the sunlight streaming in the window. For a long moment she stood looking at him, with an expression of surprise and approval. What had he done to deserve that? If he knew he'd do it all the time. Their glances locked and held for a long moment. Despite the fact that he faced a long and lonely weekend, he savored the moment of understanding they shared.

"That depends," he said at last. "I'll keep you in mind." Keep her in mind? How was he ever going to get her *out* of his mind? "Where are you going, by the way?" He tried to make it sound like an offhand question. After all, it was none of his business, but he wanted to know. He wanted to know badly.

"I'll go off and see the sights," she said. "Just as you suggested."

With who? he wanted to ask, but he bit his tongue.

"Then tonight I'm going to a folk dance," she said.

"A dance, by yourself?" He couldn't help asking. It just came out.

"No, no. With my friend Rosie. Although it's the kind of group where you can go alone. There's always someone to dance with. I belonged to one in Chicago. They're lots of fun."

"Really."

"Yes, really. I know what you're thinking. A bunch of people dressed in weird costumes jumping around the dance floor and clapping their hands to the music. But it's not like that. It takes skill and a sense of rhythm. Some of the dancers are very good. And you don't have to wear silly hats or big skirts."

"Are you one of those very good dancers?"

She shrugged lightly. "I've taken a few lessons so I can keep up. I haven't stepped on many toes."

"I'd like to see that," he said.

"You'll have to come with me someday." Suddenly her smile abruptly faded as if she was sorry she'd said that and wished she could take back her offer. "That is if you…"

"Don't feel that you have to drag me around with you," he said quickly, realizing she had spoken too quickly. "It will be a long time before I'm ready for dancing again."

"You might not enjoy it anyway."

There was an awkward silence. Each being afraid they'd stepped over the imaginary lines they'd drawn. Rahman knew they'd never go anywhere together socially. It wasn't that she was his nurse and he was her patient. It wasn't even that they came from different backgrounds. It was more than that. It was her reticence. He knew there was something she wasn't telling him. A lot of things she wasn't telling him. There was a man in her life, he was sure of that. There had to be. She was just too attractive, too capable, too lovely, too…yes, too everything to have gone unnoticed by the men in the world.

Then there was his reluctance to ever get entangled with a woman again. Not that a folk dance would lead to an entanglement, but still…he had to be careful. She had an effect on him. There was no denying that. She made him dream dreams he had no business dreaming. She also made him want to get well—fast. To show her he wasn't always like this. That was one of the good effects she had on him.

"Right," he said, wanting to let her off the hook. Truthfully he could think of nothing better than watching her spin around a dance floor. He imagined her face flushed, her skirts twirling and her hair tousled. He could almost hear the fiddles tuning up and feel the vibration from the shoes hitting the floor. He knew she'd be good at it. He also knew there would be a line of men waiting to dance with her. He felt a tight knot of jealousy behind his cracked ribs thinking of her in some strange man's arms.

"Well," she said briskly, "I'll be off now." She picked up her suitcase and without a backward glance left the room as if she didn't know what else to say and perhaps regretted saying what she'd said already.

He sat there staring at the open door of his room. Sure, the sun was still shining through the window. He was as comfortable as a man could be with his multiple injuries. But it was as if a dark cloud had settled over the room. She was gone. She said she'd come back, but what if she didn't? What if she met someone at the dance, or went back to Chicago, or found another job?

Without the need to put up a front for Amanda, he sank back onto his pillows, closed his eyes and gave in to a feeling of melancholy. A few minutes later Nurse Whitmore came into the room to give him a shot. She was brisk and efficient, but her hands were surprisingly gentle and he had to admit her technique was almost as good as Amanda's.

"How are we feeling?" she asked, after he'd turned over.

"Just great," he said, trying to suppress a sarcastic tone.

She gave him a quick glance that said she was no stranger to sarcasm and quite aware that anyone in his situation wouldn't feel great at all and pulled out a thermometer. She held it up to the light and glanced around the room. "Nice place you've got here."

"Yes, it is."

"Lucky for you you're out of the hospital."

"I know that," he said stiffly. He didn't need to be reminded how lucky he was to have enough money to afford a nice house and a private nurse. He knew that other patients were lying in their hospital beds at the mercy of the doctors' and nurses' schedules, obliged to share their care with dozens of others. It didn't do anything for the pain he was in nor the despair he sometimes felt at the long road to recovery. Or the nagging feeling that he'd been wasting his life and the worry that he might continue to do so after he was well.

When she put the thermometer into his mouth and took his pulse, he was relieved that he didn't, couldn't make any more polite conversation. He preferred to lie in his bed and sulk for a while, maybe the whole weekend. But Nurse Whitmore had other ideas.

"Wondered if you minded if I watched the golf tournament on that big screen in the den," she said, taking the thermometer out of his mouth and writing something on his chart.

"Of course not," he said. "Help yourself."

"Maybe you'd care to join me," she suggested.

"Oh, I don't think…" he said. Watching golf with a substitute nurse on a Saturday afternoon. How low could he sink? How depressing could his situation get?

"The housekeeper said you play a pretty mean game of golf yourself."

"Played," he said, emphasizing the past tense. "Yes, I did, at one time. But that was a long time ago." Actually it was last summer, but it seemed like years ago. He used to play with Rafik, then with Lisa, who played golf as she did everything else—with verve and recklessness, hitting balls into the rough, racing through eighteen holes, playing through other foursomes with her nonstop energy, taking on every and anybody who wanted to play. They also used to travel to all the major tournaments to cheer on their favorites.

He didn't picture himself ever playing again and had little desire to watch golf, especially with someone he didn't know. He would prefer to lie in bed and think of all the things he couldn't do anymore. That was the kind of mood he was in.

"Come on then," she said, holding out her arm to give him a hand out of bed and into his wheelchair.

Hadn't he just said no? He couldn't say it again without being rude and after all, maybe it was better to get out of the room and stop thinking about his limitations and about what Amanda might be doing.

Nurse Whitmore was delighted with the high resolution on the big-screen TV in the study. It seemed she was a big sports fan, not just golf, but baseball and professional football as well. "Look at that picture, would you?" she said, sitting back in a large leather chair, staring in wonder at the huge screen and the excellent clarity of the picture. "The grass is so green, you'd swear you were right there in the stands."

"Or at a sports bar," Rahman muttered under his breath but not loud enough for her to hear. He wished he could get as much pleasure out of a golf game on TV as his nurse did, or folk dancing as Amanda did. He realized that some might call him a spoiled brat, complaining about his injuries when his money and position afforded him the best care possible. Was it his fault he'd been brought up to expect the best?

He stared at the screen while he did some unaccustomed reflecting and allowed himself a few moments of introspection. Yes, he'd been born to privilege, but that didn't mean he could sit back and wait for the world to be handed to him on a silver platter. His father had said this to him many times over the years, but it had never sunk in. He was beginning to wonder what he could do to change his life.

First he had to recover. Amanda had assured him he would. Though the progress he was making seemed painfully slow. That was another thing. He'd never had much patience. When he wanted something, he wanted it now. His health wasn't coming back *now*. It was taking more time and more work on his part than he'd imagined.

Nurse Whitmore interrupted his reverie with a shout when her favorite player made a spectacular shot. He watched as she clapped her hands gleefully, totally out of character for his vision of a middle-aged nurse from the old school.

"Do you usually watch with your husband?" he asked politely during the first commercial break.

"I did," she said, and her face suddenly changed expression. She pressed her lips together for a moment as if to hold back something she didn't want to let go. "Until he died two years ago. Massive coronary while he was at work."

"I'm sorry," Rahman said. He was stuck for more words. He knew how empty they could be, how little comfort to those left behind.

She sighed and propped her feet on an ottoman. "Thirty years together. That's a long time. For a while I couldn't watch sports at all. Made me too sad. Made me think of him. You think I'm a fan?"

"Yes, I do. That's unusual for a woman," he said. Especially for a woman her age. But he didn't say that.

"You should have seen George. Glued to the tube every Sunday afternoon. I'd bring in the chips and the beer then go do something else. Then one day I sat down. 'If you can't beat 'em, then join 'em,' I said to myself, and then I really got into it. Even football. Now that he's gone, it's not the same, but…'' Her lower lip trembled and Rahman had to turn away. He tried to think of something to say. He was afraid to ask what he really wanted to know, but he did anyway.

"How did you get over his death?" he asked. Maybe this woman had the secret to recovering from tragedy. He studied her broad, lined face. There were lines there that said she'd suffered. But there was something in her eyes that looked as if she'd come to terms with it. A kind of acceptance. She looked as if she knew something he didn't.

"Time," she said. "And people. I have my daughter and grandkids. Doesn't do to be too much alone. The best part is to feel needed. That's one reason I've kept my job. Nothing like nursing to make a person feel needed.''

He nodded and the golf game came back on the air. Needed. Who needed him? He had no wife, no children, no grandchildren. His brother didn't need him anymore. His parents had each other. Time. He had time. But he was too impatient to simply wait until time eased the pain of loss.

He tried to follow the game but his attention wandered. He found himself envying the woman across the room who was rooting for one of the players. It was obvious she cared who won. He used to care. How long would it be before he cared again? About anything. About his future. About his family.

He wondered what Amanda was doing at that moment. Had she taken his advice to ride the cable car to the top of the mountain for the view? He'd love to see her face as the panorama spread out before her, the lake gleaming below, the snow glistening on the peaks in the sun as far as you could see. Was she alone? He hoped not, he didn't want her to be lonely, and yet he wanted to be the one to show it to her.

He couldn't show it to her unless he got well enough. Even if he was well enough she might not want to see it with him. She might find him uninteresting company. After spending weeks with him she might be glad to get rid of him. She might be only being nice to him because she had to. It was her job. That was a depressing thought. When she came back on Sunday night, he was going to make an effort to be more pleasant, to stop complaining, to be better company. He used to be a lot of fun. He used to be the one who made everyone else laugh. He might not have contributed much to the family business, but he could always be the life of the party.

If he could regain some of his lost personality, he might be able to entertain Amanda and win her over, as a friend of course. Only because he could use a friend. And she would be a good friend to have. But not a girlfriend. No more girlfriends. He couldn't face the loss of another one. He was simply going to expand his circle. Yes, a big crowd had gathered around his hospital bed, but he'd been in no shape to enjoy their company. He'd been relieved to see them go and they seemed relieved to be released from the duty of visiting a sick friend. A sick friend whose body was broken as well as his spirit. He hadn't heard much from any of them since.

As if on cue the telephone rang. Nurse Whitmore answered it and handed the portable phone to Rahman. It was Nicole, someone who'd been part of his crowd in San Francisco. She was one of the society girls he hung out with in the old days. A pretty blonde who had plenty

of family money and who played the field when it came
to men. She wanted to know how he'd been. He rolled
his wheelchair into the hall so he wouldn't interrupt the
nurse's golf game with his conversation.

"I'm coming up to the lake to do some skiing," Nicole said. "I thought I'd come by to see you, that is if
you're up for some company."

"Of course," he said. Maybe it would do him good
to see someone from his past now that he was feeling
better than he had in the hospital. "I'll give you direc-
tions how to get to the house."

After she had written them down he asked after a few
friends.

"Everyone's kind of drifted apart," she said. "It's not
the same without you and Lisa."

No, nothing was the same without Lisa. She was the
glue who held everything together. She was the one who
planned the trips to Las Vegas for weekends of clubbing
and gambling, who organized all the parties. He wasn't
the only one who missed her. She'd obviously left a gap
in the old gang that no one could fill.

"We were just talking about you the other night at
The Blue Dolphin. Wondering how you were, when
you'd be back. We're planning the next tailgate party
before the football game."

Rahman could picture them gathered in the parking
lot at the Forty Niners' stadium, the barbecue smoking,
everyone dressed in the team colors, drinking beer, getting so carried away, they sometimes didn't even bother
going to the game.

"Wish I could be there," he said. But he wasn't sure
he would ever be ready to rejoin the group again and

carry on as if nothing had happened. "It will be good to see you, Nicole," he said. It would be good to see her. Maybe it would help to talk about Lisa instead of trying to forget her.

Chapter Five

The music was loud, the dance floor was packed and Amanda didn't lack for partners. She had enjoyed her day off so far and now was especially enjoying being the new girl at the dance. But when the band took a well-deserved break, one of the men followed her back to her table where Rosie was waiting for her. He was a good dancer, but she had no interest in seeing any more of him. She was there to dance, not to pick up men. It didn't take more than a few minutes for the man to realize that there was no future in hitting on her. As soon as he sensed her attention was wandering, he excused himself and walked across the floor to join his friends.

"What was wrong with him?" Rosie asked with a puzzled look. "I thought he was cute."

"Nothing. He *was* cute."

"You didn't seem interested."

Amanda shook her head. "Not my type."

"What is your type?" Rosie asked.

Good question, Amanda thought. She knew what

wasn't her type. Arrogant doctors who kept their marital status a secret. Sheiks who were too rich and too spoiled for their own good. She'd made one terrible mistake by falling for the doctor, she was not going to make another by falling for an unavailable sheik. So why had she not given the nice, attractive man—who wasn't a bad dancer, either—a chance?

She didn't know. She only knew that he seemed boring. Maybe it was time she reconciled herself to boring. That is, if she wanted what Rosie had. A husband and kids. Because exciting men were usually not marriage material. Amanda was getting too old to go out just to have a good time. It was time to look for a husband.

Rosie was waiting for her answer.

"My type? I want a family man. Someone who's ready to settle down." *Not a party animal who has to be surrounded with bright lights and crowds of friends all the time.* "Who wants what I want. The rose-covered cottage and a picket fence." *Not someone who's only happy in a mansion or an estate.* "Who comes from a similar background." *Humble beginnings, not raised to wealth and position.* "Someone who doesn't come with a lot of emotional baggage." *Like a recently deceased girlfriend.*

"Well that doesn't sound too hard to find," Rosie said. "There are probably some like that in this very room."

Amanda looked around the room at the couples standing at the bar or sitting at tables taking a break from the dancing. Yes, there probably were some likely candidates right here under her nose. She ought to be looking more carefully, but she just couldn't force herself to do it. Right now it seemed like an overwhelming task.

"The problem is," Amanda admitted, leaning across

the table to confide in her friend. "That I'm not attracted to that type, the solid, sensible kind that are ready to settle down behind a white picket fence. I don't know what's wrong with me, but I always seem to fall for the ones I shouldn't."

"Oh," Rosie said. "I think I understand now. Besides everything else, there has to be an attraction. The damp palms, the shivers up the spine, the wobbly knees. That kind of thing doesn't last, you know. If it did, nobody would get any work done."

Amanda smiled. "I know that. I'm not talking about the cheap thrills. I'm talking about something else, a connection between two people, a meeting of the minds. You know what I mean, don't you? It's not just a physical attraction, though that's important, but it's more than that."

Rosie nodded slowly. "Of course I know. Don't worry, you'll find it. You'll find him. I wouldn't want you to marry anybody until you feel that spark, that connection."

"I won't, but I'm not getting any younger, Rosie. Maybe I stayed in Chicago too long."

"What was wrong with all those men in Chicago?" Rosie asked.

Which was just what Rahman had asked her. "It wasn't them, it was me," she said. "I invested too much time in someone who wasn't worth it. I'm determined not to do that again."

"Just relax and try not to worry about Mr. Right," Rosie said. "Sometimes you find what you're looking for just when you stop looking. Someone who's right around the corner. Someone you'd discounted or taken for granted. Suddenly he's right there and he's right for you."

Amanda nodded, but she didn't really believe it would be that easy. Especially if she kept making the same mistakes over again. The music started and she was out on the dance floor again trying to do what Rosie suggested. Relax and not worry about finding Mr. Right. Her real problem was a little different. It was how to keep from falling for Mr. Wrong.

After a leisurely Sunday with church in the morning followed by brunch then playing dolls with Rosie's twins in the afternoon, Amanda walked out with her friend to the low-slung red sports car parked in the driveway.

"Red looks good on you," Rosie said, standing back to admire her friend in the driver's seat of the expensive sports car.

"I'm afraid it's a little rich for my taste," Amanda said, leaning back into the comfort of the heated leather seats. "Though I think I could get used to this kind of luxury." Not only the car, but the house and the housekeeper and the furniture and just about everything else.

"Pretty nice of Rahman to lend it to you. He must trust you to hand over the keys to this baby. Come to think of it, you haven't said much about our friend the sheik this weekend," Rosie said. "I hope you know he's in good hands while you're gone. Dorothy Whitmore is an excellent nurse. She's from the old school and she won't put up with any nonsense."

"Yes, that's what I thought," Amanda said. "I appreciate your finding her. It's been good for me to get away." Yes, it was good for her to get away. But it wasn't good for her to be thinking about Rahman so much while she was away. No, she hadn't talked about him. That was a deliberate strategy. If Amanda didn't talk about him, maybe she wouldn't think about him. Unfortunately it didn't work out that way. She'd spent far too much time wondering how he was getting along with her replacement. Wondering if he was eating alone, falling into depression without her. Wondering if Dorothy Whitmore would know that he was too proud to ask for help when he needed it. Wondering if he'd be gruff and demanding. Hoping he'd been pleasant to Dorothy at least.

"Anyway, he's really been making good progress," Amanda continued. She was relieved that Rosie hadn't pressed her for any details during the weekend. Her friend was so perceptive she might guess that Amanda had mixed feelings about Rahman, feelings that disturbed her.

"That's all?" Rosie asked.

Amanda shrugged. "He has his moments. His ups and downs just like any other patient." But he wasn't like any other patient she'd ever had. His ups were such a contrast to his downs. Now that she knew he'd lost his girlfriend, she could sympathize with him. Maybe a little too much. Maybe it would be better if he wasn't sympathetic. If he was just as stubborn and difficult as she'd first thought. Better for her. Better for him.

She'd seen the look on his face when she came to his room, heard the tone in his voice, seen the way his eyes followed her around the room. It was only natural for him to form an attachment to her. It happened all the time to nurses. After all, the nurse was the only woman around day in and day out. As soon as Rahman got well, he'd be back in his element, back to the world he'd come from, the one in his scrapbook, the one that was waiting for him back in the city. The world with lots of attractive women, all eager to help him get over the one he'd lost.

As for her, she'd get another patient. Someone older this time, someone not so attractive, not so appealing, not so charming.

"I see," Rosie said. Amanda was afraid she *would* see if she said any more. Or if she stayed around much longer. She backed the car out of the driveway and waved goodbye and drove back to the house by the lake. In a funny way it seemed like coming home. As if *she'd* ever have a home like that. She was looking forward to seeing Rahman, hoping he hadn't been in a funk all weekend. Hoping he hadn't driven poor Nurse Whitmore crazy.

She let herself in the front door and was startled by the sound of loud cheers coming from the study. She rushed through the house and stood in the doorway of the book-lined study staring at the big-screen TV where huge, muscular bodies in tight-fitting uniforms were falling on top of each other. Nurse Whitmore was on her feet shouting encouragement and Rahman had raised his fist in the air and yelled, "Go Niners!" He was so excited he almost spilled the bowl of popcorn on his lap.

Amanda stood there for a long moment, speechless, unable to believe her eyes. Never in a million years would she have imagined the older, sedate white-uniformed woman to be a football fan. Nor would she have imagined that Rahman would want to spend the afternoon watching football with her. Obviously she'd misread both of them.

They were both oblivious to her presence. Amanda hadn't known what to expect upon her return, but it wasn't this. At best, she had expected to find Rahman suffering from depression in his darkened room and to find the nurse shaking her head in dismay over him. She had imagined that Nurse Whitmore would be at the door with her bag packed, watching anxiously for Amanda's return so she could escape. Instead Amanda felt like an intruder.

Amanda didn't know what to do. Even if she cleared her throat discreetly, she doubted they'd hear her over the din of the announcer's voice, their own voices and the cheers from the stadium. So she stood there and stared at the men on the huge screen, as they rammed into each other, fell down and got up again, dazed and possibly injured. She watched as they walked off the field helped by a teammate or returned to the field only to be knocked down again. She'd never watched professional football before. She considered it too violent. Today, as she watched thousands of fans in the stands, it seemed she was the only one who felt that way. Definitely the only one in this house, anyway.

She could have gone to her room. Or she could have stood there forever. Instead she edged her way into the room until they caught sight of her.

Rahman said hello as matter-of-factly as if she'd just left the room for a moment and hadn't been gone an entire weekend. So much for worrying that he'd fall into a funk without her around.

Dorothy Whitmore looked startled to see Amanda. She hit the mute button on the remote control and said hello. She glanced at her watch and said something about the time. "I'll just get my things," she said.

"You're not leaving before the end of the game, are you?" Rahman asked her.

"Well, I..."

"Please, don't leave on my account," Amanda protested.

"Well, if you're sure..." Dorothy said.

"Of course," Amanda said, backing out of the room.

"I'll just go check on some things." It was obvious she wasn't needed. She'd never seen Rahman look so well. The color was back in his face. His voice seemed stronger, though she couldn't imagine why if he'd spent all afternoon yelling at a TV screen.

Amanda went to her room and changed her clothes. Then she went to the kitchen to see what the house-keeper had left them for dinner. It was her day off, too. She found a chicken potpie—with instructions to bake it at three-hundred and fifty degrees for an hour—and a salad and another scrumptious dessert. She wondered if she should ask Nurse Whitmore to stay for dinner. While she was pondering, the nurse came to the kitchen, this time with her bag in her hand.

"I'm off," she said. "I wrote down everything on his chart. Vital signs, etcetera. He took all his meds and ate pretty good, too. Hope you had a good weekend."

"Yes, thanks," Amanda said. "I...I assume you got along all right?"

"Oh, sure. He acts like a bear at first, but underneath he's just a lamb. A real sweetheart. Yes, we got along just fine. Once I got him out of his room. Nice for me to have someone to watch the game with today. And golf yesterday. Did you know he was on his college team? Taught me a few things about birdies and bogies I didn't know."

"Well, that's good. That's fine," Amanda said, too surprised to say much else as she walked Dorothy to the front door. She still couldn't believe it. *Underneath he's just a lamb.* Was that really what she'd said? Could it be that Dorothy Whitmore understood Rahman better in one weekend than she'd been able to in all the time she'd been with him?

After she watched Dorothy pull out of the driveway,

Amanda took Rahman's medicine and a cup of water and went to the study to find him staring at the books on the shelves, lost in thought.

"How are you?" she asked, looking closely at his face and into his eyes for signs of fatigue.

"Fine," he said automatically, his mind obviously on other things. "Did you know Dorothy's husband died two years ago? They'd been married thirty years. They used to watch all the games together."

Dorothy? Amanda hid her surprise that he was calling her by her first name. "No wonder she said it was nice to have someone to watch the game with. She must miss him terribly."

He nodded. "Yes, but she has a great attitude. Do you know she'd never seen a game on a big screen? It makes a big difference," he said.

"It was so close I felt I was right there on the field," Amanda said. She gave a little shiver. She'd never understand a fascination for football.

"Too much for you?" he inquired.

"A little violent," she confessed. "I suppose you played football, too?"

"No, but I have season tickets for the Forty Niners. Though the games seemed to become an excuse to party both before and afterward. I saw more of the game today than I ever have in the actual stadium. Rafik and I avoided playing football, but we played just about everything else...golf, tennis, polo."

"You'll play again one of these days."

"Maybe. Maybe not. Rafik is too busy for sports. Maybe it's time I moved on, did something else."

She handed him his medicine which he gulped down.

"You've never told me what kind of work you do,"

she said, sitting on the edge of the armchair opposite him.

"Maybe because I do so little of it," he said.

She didn't know if he was joking or not. "But…but I understood…"

"You understood we have a successful venture company, did you? That's true. It's also true that I haven't exactly been the star performer. My grandfather started the company and made it a success. Then my father brought it to the West Coast where it's doing better than ever. Rafik has taken his place and found some ventures to invest in that are performing very well, even with the economy the way it is. I know what I have to do…it's just…"

She opened her mouth to speak, but he continued. "Don't say everything will be all right, once I get well. I was well and everything wasn't all right. I never felt comfortable in the office, especially with the portrait of grandfather on the wall of the lobby looking down at me disapprovingly as I came through the door. He always looked like he was saying, 'You'll never make it, son. You'll never be the success your father is or even your brother. You don't have the drive, the ambition.' Of course he was right."

"How can you say that?" she asked. "You're only thirty-two. Maybe he *was* right, but you have plenty of time to be as successful as your father. Even more so. If that's what you want."

"Ah, there's the question. If I want. I've never wanted it. I've never known what I wanted. But I've been thinking…"

"Yes?"

"Never mind. I don't want to bore you with my ideas. Tell me about your weekend."

"Why don't I bring in our dinner first?" she suggested.

They ate together in the study where she lit the fire that had been laid in the tiled fireplace. With the television stored out of sight, the curtains drawn and the flames dancing in the fireplace, they ate the housekeeper's flaky chicken pie on a small drop-leaf table. They sat close enough that Amanda could see the flames reflected in Rahman's dark eyes.

He seemed so different tonight. She couldn't believe he was the same person who'd been so upset that she was going to take the weekend off. Demanding to know why she needed a weekend nurse. Insisting he didn't need anybody. She kept glancing up at him to be sure he really was the same man. He'd been rejuvenated this weekend. She just didn't know how or why. She didn't want to stare at him, but she couldn't help noticing that his jaw was firmer, that he'd shaved and that his eyes were brighter. She kept trying to figure out what had happened.

Instead of her making conversation to bring him out of his shell, he took the initiative. He asked her about the folk dance. "I'll bet you didn't lack for partners. Did you meet anyone special?" he asked, setting his fork down on the table.

"I wasn't looking for anyone special," she said. As if it was any of his business who she met.

"Why not?" he asked. "Don't you want to get married and have twins like your friend Rosie?"

"All of a sudden everyone's interested in getting me married off," she said a little defensively, wondering if she'd prompted these latest remarks by looking desperate or unhappy with her lot in life. She didn't want to give anyone the impression she was the least bit concerned or even interested in marriage at this time. "There must be something in the air. Of course I want to get married someday, but I'm not sure being a good dancer correlates with anything else." She took a deep breath. "As for twins, if they were anything like you, I don't think I could handle two at a time."

She had a brief vision of two little boys who looked like Rahman and his brother, leading their elders on a merry chase. They'd live in a big house with acres of lawn and plenty of hired help. Rahman would be a doting father. She could tell by the way he interacted with Rosie's girls. She felt a stab of envy for his wife, whoever she would be. No doubt a beautiful girl who fit into the scene like someone who'd been sent by Central Casting to fill the role. The vision filled her with a painful jealousy that she'd never felt before. She was ashamed of herself.

"I'm serious," he said. "What are your plans for the future?"

She was jerked out of her reverie, but couldn't shake off the image of Rahman happily married. How she wished the table wasn't so small. She wished he wasn't so close. She wished she could plead the fifth and refuse to answer these questions on the grounds they might incriminate her. Because it was hard to answer these questions with a standard reply while he was looking at her so intently, as if he really wanted to know. As if her answer was important to him.

His dark eyes didn't leave her face. She shifted her weight and crossed her legs. She folded and refolded her napkin. She couldn't get comfortable with his steady gaze on her, waiting for her answer. Her face felt hot but her hands were cold. Her heart sped up. If she didn't know better, Amanda would have thought she was coming down with something.

She was relieved the lights were dim. She didn't want Rahman to see her cheeks flaming and guess how much his presence and his questions disturbed her. Her conversation with Rosie came back to her. If she'd had any doubt before, it was gone tonight. Yes, it was there in the air, that special spark, that electricity in the air they were talking about. She couldn't deny the physical attraction between them. But it was more than that. It was a feeling, an emotion that pervaded the room, it underlined everything they said to each other, it gave every remark a special meaning. But was she the only one who felt it? Was it important? Would it last? She knew the answer to that. It would last only as long as she was here working for him.

She stood abruptly.

"I don't have any plans except for bringing in the chocolate cake and the coffee from the kitchen."

He grabbed her arm. "Forget the cake. I can't believe there haven't been any men in your life, Amanda. What are you waiting for? Who are you looking for?" There was an urgency in his voice she couldn't ignore.

"Rosie asked me that same question yesterday," she said. "All right if you want to you. I told her I was looking for a family man, someone who's ready to settle down. Who knows what he wants and how to get it. Who would be happy in a cottage with a white picket fence." There she'd said it. She told him. Maybe it was time she put into words the thoughts that had been circulating in her brain for a long time.

"Is that so hard to find?" he asked.

"I don't know. I haven't really looked," she admitted. "I've been busy falling for men who aren't available."

"Now we're getting somewhere," he said. "Who was he?"

She sighed and sat down again. He was not going to quit until she told him. "Do you really want to know?"

"In one weekend I learned more about Mrs. Whitmore than I knew about you after two weeks. Does that seem right?" he asked.

"Let me get the coffee," she said. She had to have a break. She had to get away from him at least for a few minutes. To take a deep breath. To splash some cold water on her face and try to come to her senses.

When she came back she set the cake on the table, she felt calmer. She put another branch on the fire and poured the coffee. If she hoped he'd be distracted by the three-layer cake or the hot fragrant coffee, and forgotten his question, she was mistaken.

He took a drink of his coffee and gave her an inquiring look. "Well…" he said "…who was he?"

She stared into the flames and wondered how to explain her affair with the doctor without sounding like a complete idiot. "He," she said, "was an E.R. doctor I used to work with. He was incredibly talented, a man who could stitch up a laceration with one hand and repair a herniated disk with the other."

"So you fell in love with his ability to stitch people up?" he asked.

"I wouldn't say that," she said, with a frown. She wouldn't even say she'd fallen in love at all. Was that really love, what she'd felt for Ben? "I'd say I admired him for his skill. Everyone did. He worked twice as hard as any other physician in the place, nights, weekends, holidays and her never seemed to get tired. But there was a reason for that. I found out later he was using work as an excuse not to go home. His marriage was falling apart. He put all his energy into his work.''

"This is the man you were in love with?'' Rahman asked.

"First of all, I wasn't in love with him. I was infatuated, yes, I admit that. But I didn't know he was married. No one did. He never told me, never talked about her.''

"How long did this go on?'' Rahman asked with a frown. His cake lay on the table, untouched.

"I went out with him for about six months.''

"And you never knew he was married.'' Rahman sounded as if he didn't believe her.

"No, I told you. I would never knowingly go out with a married man. But I should have asked. I should have known. I was totally stupid. I was taken in by his charisma, his command of the emergency room. I was swept away by the attention he paid to me. I was flattered he picked me, out of all those nurses, out of all those women who were falling at his feet. Believe me, I won't make that mistake again.'' She wasn't able to suppress the bitterness in her voice.

"How did you find out?'' he asked.

"She called him on his cell phone when we were together. I put two and two together and they added up to four. I could have done it before. There were signs. I just didn't want to know. I didn't want it to end.''

"But it did end,'' Rahman said.

"Yes, right away. He couldn't deny it. He said they were going to get a divorce. But I was so devastated to find he'd lied to me I wouldn't listen. I didn't believe him about the divorce anyway. I gave my notice that day. I couldn't stand to work with him ever again. And I didn't tell anyone why I was leaving. I still haven't. I trust that you won't tell anyone either. I'm not proud of what I did. I've always believed in the sanctity of marriage. For better or worse and all that goes with it. If I thought I'd contributed to the breakup of anyone else's marriage…'' She felt hot tears sting her eyes. To think she'd been the other woman. She hated the very idea.

"It sounds as though it wasn't much of a marriage to begin with," he said.

"Maybe not," Amanda said. "But…" She couldn't speak, her throat was clogged with emotion. She could still hear the woman's voice on the other end of the phone in the distance, so distraught, so weak, so vulnerable.

Amanda thought she'd said, "Where are you?" in such a pitiful voice it almost broke her heart. Amanda could only imagine how it would feel to know your husband was having an affair with another woman. To know your marriage with the superstar of a big-city E.R., someone who looked like he was straight out of a TV drama, was falling apart. To be helpless to do anything about it.

Rahman reached for her hand across the table. The warmth of his touch was comforting and made its way to her heart. She pressed her lips together to keep from saying any more. There was a long silence in the room broken only by the crackling of the dry wood in the fireplace.

"So you came to California because of him."

"Yes." She gripped his hand tightly. "I had to get away, far away. Rosie had been asking me to come, so I did. I didn't mean to ever tell anyone about this," she said. "I certainly didn't intend to burden you with my problems."

"I'm flattered that you confided in me," he said in a

low voice that sent a wave of heat to flood her body. "Your secret is safe with me." He brought her hand to his lips and pressed his mouth against her palm. She felt her whole body flood with heat.

The warmth of his lips against her sensitive skin and the look in his eyes caused her to feel like a volcano was smoldering inside her. The lava was melting a cold lump of shame somewhere deep in her heart. Maybe she shouldn't have, but she felt sure that he meant what he said. Though she'd been determined to keep it to herself, she felt better for having told someone at last. Yet, despite the heat inside her, she was shaking all over.

It was strange, but by finally telling someone else she'd cut the pain and the disgrace in half. But why him? Why Rahman? Why not Rosie or someone else? Maybe because she didn't really know Rahman. Maybe because their relationship was short-term by its very definition. They would be together for a few more weeks and then she'd never see him again.

Then there was the fact that he'd confided in her. She knew he'd been through a tragedy, lost his girlfriend to an unexpected death and was still suffering. Maybe she owed him the truth about her own background in exchange for his confidence in her. Whatever it was, she felt a sense of relief that someone else knew the truth.

She took a deep breath and pulled her hand away in an effort to get back to normal, whatever that was. "Enough of that," she said. "I want to tell you I took your advice and went to the top of the mountain. It was beautiful, just beautiful. I took lots of pictures to send back to my friends. Maybe then they'll understand why I came out here." She took a large bite of chocolate cake and despite her emotional upheaval, she savored the rich buttery frosting.

He nodded, his dark gaze holding a wealth of understanding. She was hoping to change the subject, to get away from anything personal, but nothing seemed to work. The more she talked, the more everything she said seemed personal and had something to do with Rahman. When she saw the photos she'd taken today, would she remember that he'd been the one to recommend the view to her? Was she in some kind of danger here, the out of the frying pan type of danger? No, it wasn't possible.

When he recovered, which hopefully wouldn't be too far in the future, he'd go his way and she'd go hers. No matter how hard it would be to say goodbye. He was special, no doubt about that. Strangely enough it was he who'd made her feel worthwhile and whole again. Hopefully she'd done the same for him. But there would be no reason to ever see him again. She'd miss him. Of course she would. She'd never have another patient like him. She'd never meet another sheik.

"You look tired," he said.

"Me?" She'd been so involved in her own story she'd forgotten about him. Her patient. If anyone was tired, he must be him. "What about you? I imagine all that football wore you out. If you're finished eating, I'll take you back to your room."

He nodded.

"What else happened this weekend?" she asked while she helped him into his bed.

"Not much. Oh, a friend called. She's coming up to ski this week and she's coming by."

"That's good," Amanda said. "It will be good for you to see an old friend."

But she felt a stab of jealousy. She had no idea if this "she" meant anything at all to Rahman. Probably not. After all, he was still grieving for his lost love. It would be good for him to take an interest in someone else. She had no right to feel anything by happy for Rahman. She must stifle any other kind of unbecoming feelings.

"You'll have to be sure and invite her to dinner. I'm sure Clarice will be happy to show off her talent in the kitchen to your friend."

"I'll do that," he said. "And I want you to meet her. I'm sure she'll enjoy meeting you."

"Oh, don't worry about me," Amanda protested. "I wouldn't dream of intruding. I'll have dinner in my room and watch TV."

He didn't say anything. He didn't insist she join them. Of course not. This was a social occasion and Amanda was the nurse, not a part of his real world. The world he should be getting back to. The world he would be getting back to, very soon. Which he reminded her just before she closed his bedroom door.

"Amanda?"

"Yes?"

"What would you think if I doubled my therapy sessions. I've been slacking off. Do you think I could get better twice as fast, be out of here twice as soon if I worked twice as hard?"

"I...I don't know." She hadn't realized he'd been slacking. He looked really tired after each session. But it wasn't up to her to stifle any urge to get well faster. "Let's speak to Heidi when she comes tomorrow."

"Good," he said and gave her a smile.

She closed the door and walked slowly down the hall to her room. What had happened to make him so eager to get well faster? Was it the weekend away from her? Had she not been able to motivate him the way Nurse Whitmore had? Or was it the woman friend who was coming to see him? She knew she should feel proud of him, she wanted to feel excited that he'd turned a corner, changed his attitude, and was now really on his way to recovery. Instead she felt only puzzled and letdown. Extremely unbecoming feelings for a nurse. Feelings she would die before letting anyone see. She'd never been possessive about a patient before. What on earth was wrong with her?

Chapter Six

Rahman was exhausted after his morning workout with Heidi. He had returned to his room and was waiting for the housekeeper to bring lunch in for him and for Amanda. As tired as he was, his chest aching with every breath he took and with every muscle crying out for relief, he was still determined to step up the program. He told himself he'd feel better after lunch. Instead of a nap, he was determined to go back to the therapy room. Heidi said he could try to do more, but she looked dubious. So did Amanda. But he couldn't, wouldn't continue to be an invalid. He had to get back on his feet, however painful it would be. He had to return to the real world. To compete in business, sports, and in every other way.

He couldn't get his conversation with Amanda out of his mind. Her qualifications for a husband were stuck in his brain. She sure had thought it out though he'd had to dig some to get her to confide in him. At least he knew what she was looking for. *Someone who knows what he wants and how to get it. A family man. White picket fence.*

Those qualifications certainly let him out. He didn't know what he wanted nor how to get it. He was certainly not a family man. His family was disgusted with him. As for the white picket fence, that wouldn't be a problem. All he'd have to do would be to pick up the phone and order one. He wasn't sure why that was important to her.

It didn't matter anyway. He couldn't live up to her standards. He didn't want to. He didn't even want to get married. It just annoyed him that he wouldn't even have a chance, even if he'd wanted to. Which he didn't. That didn't mean he didn't have to get well. Now. Immediately. Or as soon as possible.

The phone rang and he picked it up from his bedside table. A man asked for Amanda. A stab of jealousy hit him between his shoulder blades like a knife. Was it someone she'd met at that dance? He didn't know what to do. Usually she answered on one of the extensions. He pushed the buzzer at his bedside, but she didn't respond.

"Can I take a message?" he asked.

"Tell her it's Ben," he said brusquely. "Dr. Sandler. It's about coming back to work. Have her call the hospital. She knows the number."

Rahman hung up and clenched his hands into tight fists. He knew without a doubt this was the man she'd told him about. The doctor with the authoritative manner. It was all there in his voice. It said he was used to giving orders and having them followed. Would Amanda be able to resist? He remembered Dorothy Whitmore saying how important it was to feel needed. This Dr.

Sandler certainly sounded like he needed Amanda. But did her need her professionally or personally, or both?

When Clarice came in and left his lunch on a tray for him on his bed and set another tray on the desk for Amanda, he asked a little more impatiently than he'd meant to where Amanda was.

"She's coming, she's coming. Don't get all upset," she said with a stern look.

"I'm not upset," he protested. "I just wondered. I don't want to start without her. We wouldn't want this delicious-looking soup to get cold, would we?" he asked, holding his spoon in the air.

"And don't think you can flatter me into ignoring your behavior, Mr. Rahman. I'm on to you, don't forget that."

"You've been on to me since I was old enough to enter the kitchen and beg for a cookie," he said. "What about my behavior? Haven't I improved any?" he asked.

"Since you were five?" She put her hands on her hips and surveyed him with narrowed eyes. "Yes, maybe a little. But you've still got a long way to go."

Rahman nodded. He knew she was right. Clarice's opinion meant a lot to him. If she didn't see any improvement in his attitude or his actions, who would?

"I'm working on it," he said as Amanda came in the door.

"What is it you're working on?" she asked when Clarice went back to the kitchen.

"My attitude, my behavior, you name it, I'm working on it. According to Clarice, I've got a long way to go."

"She has high standards," Amanda noted, sitting at the desk and crumbling a cracker into her soup.

"So do you," he said. "What is it you said you were

looking for again? A white-picket fence and a family man?''

"You asked me so I told you," she said. "I didn't expect you to bring it up again. It's not something I think about. I don't go around with a checklist. Besides, those aren't high standards, they're just personal preferences."

"Does that mean you might relax some of those requirements?" he asked.

"I suppose if there were extenuating circumstances," she said.

He watched her sip her soup and wondered what those circumstances might be. What would make up for of some of the qualities she was looking for. "Such as?" he asked.

"This is ridiculous," she said. "You're making me sound like some kind of nut, some kind of idealist. I'm sure I'll know what I'm looking for when I find it. Until then I don't intend to go out looking. Anymore than you're looking, or are you?"

"Me?" he said. He didn't want to think about his qualifications for a wife. It was entertaining and enlightening to quiz her but he didn't want the tables turned on him. He didn't want to undergo any more introspection than he already had. He knew of one way to change the subject.

"By the way, you had a call," he said. "Just a short time ago. It was a doctor. Let's see, I wrote it down somewhere."

Her face paled. She sat very still while he fumbled for the scrap of paper he'd jotted the name down, as if he'd forgotten it. He remembered exactly. "Dr. Sandler. Is that…is that the guy you were telling me about?"

She nodded. "What did he want?" she asked tersely.

"He said it's about coming back to work," he said,

watching her face closely. She wouldn't, she couldn't leave him and go back to Chicago, could she? No, of course not. But that didn't mean she wouldn't go back the minute she was finished here.

"What did you tell him?" she asked. She stood up and went to Rahman's bedside, her lunch forgotten on the desk.

"Nothing. Just that I'd give you the message." He held the paper out and she took it from his hand. "He wants you to call him."

She frowned. "I hope you didn't tell him I would."

"I didn't tell him anything. I'm just the guy who takes the messages."

Her lips curved in a slight smile. Did that mean she wouldn't go running back to Chicago? Did it mean she might not even call him back? Did that mean she felt something, anything, for him? His hopes soared.

"I don't know how he got this number," she murmured, her forehead furrowed. "He has a lot of nerve calling me."

"He sounded pretty desperate."

"Of course. He would." She stared at the phone number in her hands. He wondered if she'd tear it up right there and then. He held his breath, waiting, wondering.

"Aren't you going to finish your lunch?" he asked.

"I'm not hungry," she said stiffly. "If you still want to do more therapy this afternoon, I'm ready."

Rahman was exhausted, but he couldn't back down now. They went back into the rehab room Heidi had set up and he worked out, back and forth on the parallel bars, stretching with a giant rubber band, then she iced down his muscles while he lay on the treatment table dressed only in boxer shorts.

He'd gotten over feeling embarrassed having her see

him half dressed, seeing his bruised body. He loved the
touch of her hands on his skin. When Heidi did it, he
felt nothing. But with Amanda…it was a different story.
He could only imagine, though he had no right to, what
kind of a lover she'd be. Gentle, skillful and sensuous.
It was a good thing he was lying facedown on the table.
He was breathing hard and reacting to her touch in a
noticeable way.

"What's wrong?" she asked.

"Nothing. Just a little out of breath. You're really
working me hard."

"I thought that was what you wanted," she said.

"I did, I did. The sooner I get well, the sooner you'll
be free to go back to Chicago."

"I'm not going back. I thought I'd made that clear,"
she said.

"But if you're needed…"

"They can get someone else. No one's indispensable.
Especially not me. Just see how well you did with Dorothy Whitmore."

"I don't agree. Oh, Dorothy is a fine nurse and a good
person. But there is no one like you. Don't you know
that by now?"

Amanda didn't say anything. He was a master at flattery, when he wanted to be. But one couldn't take him
seriously. Clarice knew that and turned the tables on
him. Amanda should do the same. She kept working on
Rahman's muscles with her hands. Under the bruises and
the healing lacerations, he had a beautiful body. How
many other women had admired it under very different
circumstances, she wondered. And how many more
women would come and go out of his life before he
settled down? He seemed to have no interest in getting

married. No, he was just what he'd seemed when she'd first heard about him—a rich playboy.

Her mind was spinning. Since she got word that Ben had called she'd been thinking about the Emergency Room, about the high level of energy there, the tension, the nonstop action. Sirens screaming, ambulances arriving, patients being wheeled in. Split-second decisions being made. Did she miss it? Could she go back? Would she go back?

She glanced out the window at the snow-covered hills in the distance, with the winter sun setting behind them and knew the answers were no, no and no. She didn't know if she'd stay at Lake Tahoe, but she knew that she couldn't go back to St. Vincent's. It was partly her aversion to facing Ben again, but it was more than that. It was a chapter in her life that was closed. It was time to move on. She didn't know where she would go from here, but she knew she would not go backwards.

"Amanda?" Rahman's voice interrupted her reverie.

She'd been so engrossed in her own thoughts, she'd almost forgotten about him. "Sorry," she said. "I think that's enough for today."

When she'd pushed him back to his room in his wheelchair, she went into his bathroom and turned on his shower for him.

"When the doctor comes tomorrow," he said as she helped him take off his shirt. "I'm going to ask him what my timetable is. He's always been so vague before, but I have to know. Not only for my sake, but for yours. You don't want to spend any more of your life stuck up here taking care of me. You have opportunities, things you want to do. If it isn't going back to Chicago…"

"It isn't," she said. That was one thing she knew for sure.

"Then it will be something else. Rehab must be one of the more boring jobs for a nurse after the excitement of the E.R."

"I was ready for a change," she said. What else could she say? Being here with him in this beautiful house in this gorgeous natural setting had been more than nice. It had been an eye-opener. It had given her a chance to see how the other half lives. How wealth and position come with very special problems—living up to the expectations of successful parents and carrying on traditions. It had been a time for her to recuperate, to enjoy the kind of luxury she would never be able to afford.

On the other hand, it had made her want things she couldn't have. It had made her wish she could have met Rahman under different circumstances. To him, she'd always be his nurse, nothing more, nothing less. A person he employed like Clarice or his secretary at his office. He liked her and she liked him. He appreciated the work she did. Occasionally there was more there between them. A kind of understanding that went beyond their roles as patient and nurse.

Then there was the way he made her feel—important, skillful, soft and strong at the same time, hot and cold at the same time and above all, feminine. She sometimes wondered what would have happened if she'd been a debutante and they'd met at a party in San Francisco. Would he have asked for her phone number? Would that electricity she felt in the air have ignited sparks between them that neither could deny?

While he showered, she sat at the desk in his room filling out his chart with the pertinent data—the progress he'd made and the medicine he'd taken, so everything would be in order when the doctor came by to see him. She could hear the water running in the bathroom and she forced herself to concentrate on the chart on the desk instead of imagining how the water was running down his shoulders, how the drops might roll down his chest down…down…

She had to put the pen down when the images in her mind became too graphic. His well-formed muscles, getting firmer with every day of therapy, his bronzed skin, his bones that were mending had all become all too familiar to her. Maybe he was right. He had needed an older nurse, someone who could distance herself from her patient. Who could look at him as a patient and nothing more. It was not his fault. Just because he looked at her with those somber dark eyes as if she meant more to him than just a nurse. She didn't. It was just his way. He couldn't be around a woman without flirting with her. He even flirted with Clarice. It didn't mean anything.

When he came limping out of the shower in his terry-cloth robe using a walker, she glanced up for only a moment but that was all it took. She'd seen how his damp hair fell across his forehead and how his high cheekbones seemed more prominent, how the lines around his mouth had tightened as he made his way across the floor. She wanted to jump up and throw her arms around him and help him to his bed. But she knew he needed to do as much as he could by himself. She also knew how much she needed to be needed—especially by him. She gripped the edge of her chair to keep from getting up to help him.

"I put out some clean clothes for you," she said. "If you need some help…"

"I can manage," he said.

She nodded and discreetly and quietly left the room. When she came back he was fumbling with the buttons on his shirt and swearing under his breath. The hair on his chest was still damp. She tore her eyes away. But it was too late. Her heart was pounding. Her mouth felt like it was full of cotton balls.

"All right," he said gruffly. "I do need help."

Buttoning his shirt brought her entirely too close to him. She could smell the soap on his skin and inhale the masculine essence of the man. Her fingers were shaking so badly it took her ages to work her way down the shirt.

"Is something wrong?" he asked, his voice so deep and low and so concerned it made her knees weak.

She shook her head. She wanted to tell him that nothing was wrong except she was only human. She'd arrived at his house to take this job in a very vulnerable state. She'd been suffering from the shock of finding out she'd been taken advantage of and lied to. Now she was in danger of something even worse than falling in love with a married doctor, and that was falling in love with a patient. Not just any patient, but one who was rich and titled.

Love? What was she thinking? No, this wasn't love. This was infatuation, but just as painful and just as impossible. She willed herself to be strong, to be calm and focused. Finally she completed buttoning his shirt. She meant to step back, but before she could, he put his arms around her. She was surprised at the strength in his grip and alarmed at her response.

Instead of making some bright remark and moving away she put her arms around his neck and looked into his eyes. That was all it took. The mesmerizing look in his eyes that said he wanted her as much as she wanted him and caused her to melt in his arms. Her heart was hammering, she was trembling all over. There was so much in his dark gaze, so many questions and the answers were all yes, yes, yes.

Instead of speaking, she angled her face for the kiss she knew was coming. She knew it was coming, but she wasn't prepared for the passion it ignited. With one hand he pressed her so close to him her breasts were pressed against his hard chest muscles. His other hand cupped the back of her head and his fingers tangled in her hair. Her heart banged against her chest so loudly he must have heard it. Her whole body was on fire.

He kissed her again and again, each kiss deeper and deeper—more profound, as if he couldn't get enough of her. She felt the same, her desire blotting out everything else, all sense of propriety. She wanted him, he wanted her. Nothing else mattered. Until she realized that it did matter. Like an alarm bell ringing somewhere in the depths of her subconscious, she remembered who she was and why she couldn't do what she was doing. She pulled out of his arms and he staggered back toward his bed.

She reached for the edge of the desk and held on tightly so she wouldn't collapse.

"Are you all right?" she asked shakily.

He sat on the edge of his bed and stared at her. "Fine," he said. "I didn't mean for that to happen."

"I know you didn't," she said. Why did it hurt so much to hear him say it? Was it because even though she didn't mean for it to happen, either, she wanted it to happen. "I...I apologize. That was most...unprofessional of me."

"It wasn't your fault," he said. "It was mine."

"We'll just pretend it never happened," she said. She might pretend it hadn't happened, but she'd never forget it *had* happened.

"Good idea," he said, his face a mask of conflicting emotions. She didn't know what he was really feeling. Maybe it was best she didn't. Maybe it was best she didn't know how much he regretted his actions. That he'd been overwhelmed by emotion, a momentary feeling that he couldn't resist but that was gone now. A brief flare of passion that he'd given in to and was sorry for now that it was over.

She was sorry, too, but for different reasons. She was sorry for the lapse in her professional behavior. She was sorry for giving in to all those pent-up feelings. It was her fault for ever taking this job. She should have known it would lead to something like this. He was just too attractive to resist and he was too lonely to resist falling for the nurse. He would have fallen for whoever was with him night and day. Well, maybe not Nurse Whitmore, but anyone in his age bracket with a decent brain and body. No, it had nothing to do with her personally. The sooner she got that in her mind, the better.

"I'll take the things back to the kitchen," she said. "Are you sure you're all right?" she asked anxiously. His face was flushed and he seemed to be breathing a little faster than normal. But then, so was she.

He nodded. "What about you?" he asked.

"Of course."

"Have you made that call yet?" he said. He didn't need to say what call he was referring to.

"No."

The unspoken questions hung in the air. Will you make the call? What will you say? She didn't have the answers to either one. That was why she hadn't done it yet.

"I'm beat," he said. "You've worked me too hard this morning. I'm going to take a nap."

She nodded. As she was about the close the bedroom door behind her, she turned back to look at him. He was staring out the window, the lines of fatigue etched in his face, his eyes fixed on a faraway object. She stood there for a long moment watching him, still breathing hard, still feeling like she was on fire, her heart beating so loudly she was glad he couldn't hear it. A wave of sadness hit her. He'd already forgotten what had happened here. Though it rocked her to the soles of her feet, it was just another episode in his recuperation. That was good. Good for him, that was. Soon he wouldn't need her. That was good, too. But it was going to take some getting used to.

The next day the doctor came by. He said he was amazed at how much progress Rahman had made. He changed the drainage tubes in his chest and gave Rahman the go-ahead to do more walking on the training stairs. He said Rahman's anklebone was mending nicely.

"You've done miracles," he said in front of Rahman.

Rahman shot her a look that was full of hidden meaning. There was a glimmer in his eyes that told her he hadn't forgotten what had happened the day before and that if there was a miracle, it had something to do with her kiss.

"I haven't done anything," she protested, more for Rahman's benefit than the doctor's. "It's Rahman. He's been very determined to improve."

"Amanda inspired me," he said. "Clarice yelled at me and Nurse Whitmore forced me out of my funk. But Amanda made me want to get well. Soon. She made me want to get back to normal. To do what I used to do. To be what I used to be." Every word had a special meaning. So did his steady gaze. They'd both pointedly avoided the subject of the kisses from the day before, but now in front of the doctor, it was unspoken, but it was out in the open between them. After the doctor left, it would be swept under the carpet again, forgotten again, at least by him. As for her, it was going to take some time and a lot more effort to forget what had happened between them.

Amanda blushed hotly at Rahman's tribute to her. The doctor looked at her inquiringly. Thank heavens he had no idea what Rahman was referring to. She didn't know what to say. The doctor was no doubt wondering what her secret was. How she'd inspired him. What had she done? What had she said? She shrugged, hoping he wouldn't guess.

"How long, Doctor?" Rahman asked. "How much longer do I have to stay here?"

Amanda's heart fell. That was all he really cared about. His life here was so dull, he could hardly wait to leave. His kissing her yesterday was a way of relieving the tedium of daily life here. That was all. She told herself his was a healthy response. She told herself it was part of the process. So what if he broke her heart along the way? She knew what she had gotten into. She didn't have to be a part of it.

"At the rate you're going? A few more weeks."

He nodded and smiled. "That's good news."

When the doctor left, Rahman wheeled himself back into his room as if he wanted to show her how much he didn't need her.

"Tomorrow I want to get a computer," he said. "And set up an office in here."

"Here? Why don't you wait until you get back to the city?"

"No. I don't want to go back until I've got something to show for myself."

"I hope you're not rushing back to work too soon," she cautioned.

"Back?" he asked sharply. "I can't go back to work because I wasn't really ever there. The question isn't whether it's too soon. It's whether it's too late. I have to find out what it is I'm supposed to be doing. And I have to do it now."

"Your father will be pleased," she said.

"I suppose he will," he said. "But that's not why I'm doing it. I've been wasting my life. As Clarice has pointed out to me more than once, it's time I grew up."

Amanda was surprised to hear him being so self-critical. But pleased to see him taking action. Just as she'd surmised, he didn't say another word about her effect on him, or what that brief embrace had meant to him. She knew why. It had meant nothing.

They had a lot of work to do together during the next few days—ordering the equipment, installing another phone line, a fax machine and a copier and getting everything ready for business. They were each extremely careful not to come into close physical proximity with each other, as if just a touch might set off another explosion that neither one wanted nor would be able to put out this time. The tension in his room was palpable. Of course he was tense about starting his business. And she was more than tense about stepping over the bounds of her job. He wanted her advice. He wanted her help. But she was just a nurse. She had no idea of how to set up an office.

She stood in the middle of his bedroom/office looking at the new shelves, the desk and the equipment. Rahman was sitting in his wheelchair looking excited and apprehensive at the same time.

"What do you think?" he asked Amanda with a trace of anxiety in his voice.

"I think it's amazing," she said. What she really thought was that he was amazing to have done it all so quickly. Of course he had the money to buy whatever he wanted, but he still had to make many decisions and make them quickly. He'd done it all on the phone, urging haste and making snap decisions which took skill. "But I'm wondering what will happen when you leave and go back to your office in the city. Won't all this stuff just sit here unused?"

"Not at all. I'll be back from time to time. So will other family members. A home office is the latest thing. Adds a lot of value to a house. I'm surprised you don't know that, Amanda." The words might have been offensive, but the teasing grin on his face told her how much he liked to push her buttons to see if he could get a rise out of her.

"That's the nice thing about being a nurse," she said. "I learn something new every day."

"I hope I can continue to contribute to your expanding bank of knowledge," he said with a gleam in his eye.

"I'm sure you can," she said. She recognized that everything he said had a dual meaning. Especially when accompanied by that look in his eye.

She turned away, pretending interest in the scanner he'd just bought.

"Now I have to make some calls," he said. She took the hint, left the room immediately and went to the kitchen to see Clarice. She was chopping vegetables for a stew. Amanda asked if she could help. Not only had she learned a few things from Rahman, it wouldn't hurt to learn a few culinary secrets from the housekeeper who was one of the best cooks she'd ever encountered.

"Well, sure, if you want to," Clarice said, handing a cleaver to Amanda. "How's he doing?"

"I'm afraid he's overdoing it trying to double his therapy while setting up this office and plunging into a new business venture. He's just finished overseeing the installation of all this new equipment, the computer, the printer, the new desk and the storage cabinets. But whenever I suggest he rest, he's refused."

"Seems happier than I've seen him in years," Clarice observed, popping a chunk of carrot into her mouth.

"Really?" Despite his obvious fatigue from time to time, Amanda had been surprised at how easy Rahman was to deal with. There had been dozens of decisions to be made. Though she'd never had any experience in setting up a home office or getting a foot into the business world, he sometimes wanted to talk over the options with her. When he listed the pros and cons, they'd inevitably come to the same conclusion. Just from watching him work through these problems and hearing him on the telephone, she could see that he had the intelligence and the perception to be a success at whatever he did. All he'd needed was the motivation. She still didn't know where it had come from. She couldn't believe he really owed it to her.

"Yes," Clarice said. "I confess I've been worried about him. Especially after Rafik got married and settled down, both in his home life and at the office. Suddenly there was only one black sheep instead of two. I had the feeling he was trying to live up to his reputation as the only remaining bad boy of the family by being even worse. I knew he had it in him to be a success, but I didn't know what it would take to turn things around. You've been good for him, you know.''

"That's what the doctor said," Amanda said, adding a pile of chopped celery to the large bowl of onions and carrots. "But I haven't done anything much, just what any other nurse would have done in my place." She could have bitten her tongue off. A flare of heat suffused her body. She knew perfectly well no other nurse would have succumbed to Rahman's advances. Even if she'd been tempted, any other nurse would have been able to control herself. She had a horrible feeling that Clarice could see into her mind and knew what she'd done. That she'd violated every rule in the nurse's handbook.

"Not so," Clarice said, apparently oblivious to Amanda's reaction to her own words. "You've had an effect on him that no one has ever had before. He likes you, he respects you and he wants your approval, maybe he wants even more from you. I don't know how you'd feel about that." Clarice slanted an inquiring glance in Amanda's direction.

Amanda tried to make her face into a mask of discretion. She hoped that Clarice wouldn't see the swirling emotions and the shame that lurked. She wanted to protest what she'd said about her having an effect on him that no one else had had. She was afraid she was just another flirtation in a list of many that had come before her.

She didn't know what to say to Clarice, so she didn't say anything. She didn't want to disagree, but she was sure Rahman didn't want anything from her except her abilities to help him get well. Instead she asked how long the meat should brown before putting it in the oven and the conversation switched to a much safer subject. Soon the kitchen was filled with the homey and comforting smells of roasting vegetables and meat and simmering broth.

"You're the one who's made him recover faster," Amanda said. "Who wouldn't get stronger with all this delicious food coming out of your kitchen every day? I think I've gained ten pounds since I've been here."

Clarice smiled modestly and patted Amanda on the shoulder. "You can use the extra pounds," she said. "I thought when you came you looked awfully peaked. Both of you have sure spruced up. If I've had any part in that, I'm proud," she said.

Amanda and Clarice exchanged smiles. They both wanted the best for Rahman. The difference was Clarice would be around to see the outcome, to follow Rahman's progress over the years, but Amanda wouldn't. She'd be...where? She had no idea. She envied the older woman. Envied her for being a part of the family— trusted, loved, respected. She also admired her for being more than just a cook. She'd been a strong influence on Rahman.

"Now," Amanda said as Clarice began mixing flour and butter together. "Tell me your secret for light, flaky biscuits."

When she returned to Rahman's room she found he was immersed in his new business. He had his new desk where he could wheel himself up to it and swing into a swivel chair. He was studying the words on the computer screen. When Amanda came in, he swiveled around and grinned at her as if he'd accomplished something special. He had.

"What do you think?" he asked.

She returned his smile. "You look like you know what you're doing."

His smile faded. "But I don't. Not really. Oh, I've

gotten started. But every time I look up, I wonder if maybe you're right. Maybe I went overboard on the equipment. Maybe I should have waited until I got back to the city. What have I done, Amanda?''

"Can't you call your father, ask him what to do?"

Suddenly his attitude changed. He sat up straight despite the pain in his chest and squared his shoulders. His jaw was firm, his gaze steady. "Of course I could, but I'm not going to. That's not the point. The point is for me to think of what to do and then surprise him with the results." He turned back to the computer, tapped his fingers against the desk, then looked at her over his shoulder. "Are you going to just stand there? Don't you have something to do?"

"I have been doing something," she said, stung by his words. "I've been learning how to make biscuits."

Chapter Seven

Rahman nodded, but she could tell his mind was elsewhere and she was glad. Amanda realized that she could be no more help to him in this new endeavor. No one could. Not her, not his father and not his brother. He had to do this himself. She could tell he was nervous and worried about failing. He didn't want any witnesses if he did. But he wouldn't fail. He had all the right instincts and the courage and all the resources he wanted. She should have told him that. But he might have taken it the wrong way. He didn't need a pep talk. She was confident he was ready to take on the world. She just hoped his body was as ready as his spirit.

She stood in the living room looking out the window at the gray skies and softly falling snow. Rahman wasn't the only one who had to decide what to do. With her job ending in a few weeks, it was time for her to take steps to move on. First she had to call Ben. With any luck, she'd get his voice mail and she wouldn't have to talk to him. She'd leave a message. The message would say she wasn't coming back. Then she wouldn't have to argue with him. But she didn't get his voice mail. She got him.

"Amanda," he said. "I was afraid you weren't going to call back." He sounded anxious, almost unsure. Very unlike the confident, self-assured surgeon she knew. It made it harder to think of how to counter his arguments that were sure to come. "It's so good to hear your voice," he continued. "I can't tell you how much I've missed you. But not just me. The patients have missed you and the rest of the staff. I was afraid you hadn't gotten my message."

She gripped the phone tightly with icy fingers. She'd need all the strength she could get to turn him down. *The patients have missed you.* How like him to try to make her feel guilty.

"Yes, I got it. I'm only calling to say no," she said, proud of how steady and cool her voice was.

"You're not serious," he said. "How can you be happy doing private duty in some backwater when you're the greatest E.R. nurse St. Vincent's has ever had?"

"Come on, Ben. I'm sure you can find someone to take my place."

"We found someone, but she left when she got a better offer somewhere else. Frankly we were glad to see her go. She just didn't have what it takes. What you have. Nerves of steel, calm under fire, steady hands, cool head…warm heart."

He said the last words so softly she might have imagined them. She hoped she had imagined them. She no longer had a warm heart where Ben Sandler was concerned. When she left Chicago her heart felt like it was frozen. She had shut off that part of her anatomy, maybe for good. Maybe she would never be able to love again, or trust again, or believe anyone who told her he loved her. Why should she? It was safer that way.

"How are you doing?" he continued. "I don't mean the job. I mean, how are you really?"

"I'm fine, just fine," she said. "For your information, this is not some backwater. This is a beautiful Alpine village with snow-covered mountains and a pristine lake. Mark Twain thought Lake Tahoe was the fairest sight in the whole earth. People come from all over the world to ski here."

"I didn't know you skied," he said.

"I don't. Not yet. But I'm thinking of taking it up." She hadn't actually thought of taking it up, but if she stayed…

"Really?" he said with a hint of skepticism in his voice.

"Yes, really. Now I really have to go. Good luck, Ben," she said. And hung up.

"You're quiet tonight," Rahman said over their dinner of savory beef stew and hot biscuits.

"Sorry," she said. "I was just thinking."

"Would you like to share your thoughts?" he asked, buttering a biscuit. He was so pleased with the work he'd done that afternoon, he felt positively delirious. Delirious and ravenous. He hadn't been really hungry since before the accident. He thought he'd never tasted anything as good as the flaky biscuit that seemed to melt in his mouth. Every one of his senses was sharpened, heightened. Every time he looked across the table at Amanda he drew in a breath of pleasure. She was so beautiful it made his heart ache in a way that had nothing to do with his injuries. He'd shared so much with her.

They'd been through so much together. Yes, he wanted to get well so he could get on with his life, but how was he going to get on with it without her?

He'd had a hard time restraining himself since the day he'd lost control and kissed her. He thought it would be good for him to give in and do what he'd wanted to do since the first time she stood in the doorway of his hospital room. It was good for him in some ways, in others it had only made him want more. Want to see what would happen if he took it to a new level.

He wanted to make love to her, to feel her soft skin next to his, to feel her legs wrapped around his waist, to hear her call his name at the moment of ecstasy, to exchange the deepest and most profound feelings any two people could. He didn't for a moment think she'd go that far, at least not while he was her patient. But what about later? He studied her face, loving the way her hair curled against her cheek, then his eyes fixed on her mouth, remembering how sweet her kisses were.

Maybe it was selfish of him, but he wanted to share everything with her. His excitement with his new enterprise and his disappointment if it didn't work out. All this he wanted her to share with him. If Amanda was unhappy, he wanted to know why. He wanted to do something about it. She'd been so patient with him, throughout all his low moments, where he didn't seem to be getting well and didn't care if he did or not, he owed her the same concern she'd showed him.

"Share my thoughts? Not really," she said. "They're not really worth sharing."

"Did you call the doctor?" he asked.

She winced and Rahman felt a flash of anger toward a man he didn't know and didn't want to know. The doctor had said something that had disturbed her. He wished now he hadn't given her the message.

"What did he say to upset you?" he asked, clenching his hands into fists.

"Nothing," she said. "He asked me to come back and I said no."

"Just like that?" he asked. He couldn't believe it had been that simple. "Did he try to twist your arm?"

"He tried to make me feel guilty for deserting all those patients who need me."

"Did you tell him how much I need you? How I would never have gotten well without you?"

She shook her head. "You would have gotten well without me. All you had to do was to change your attitude. That had nothing to do with me."

He almost blurted out the truth. It had everything to do with her. He wanted to get well so he could get to know her on equal footing. He wanted her to see him as a man who was in charge. The next time he kissed her, he wanted her to know he was a man who knew what he wanted and how to get it. The kind of man she was looking for.

He studied her face. He didn't know what was wrong but he knew it was something. He was so keyed up tonight he wanted to share the joy. But she wasn't in the mood. Not that she seemed unhappy, just pensive. As usual, he had a hard time figuring her out.

"Great biscuits," he said for lack of anything better. "Did you say you'd made them?"

"I helped. Cooking is very therapeutic."

"He upset you, didn't he? That's why you need therapy. How could he have the nerve to make you feel guilty, to ask you to go back there, after what he did to you?" He was so angry the blood rushed to his face.

"He's not coming here to try to persuade you, is he? Because if he did, I wouldn't be able to control myself. If he was here right now, I might punch him in the mouth."

She stared at him. Was she revolted at his thoughts of violence? "Fortunately that won't be necessary," she said. "In your condition, you might do more damage to yourself than to him."

"Even in my condition, I seem to be able to rise to the occasion," he said. She gave him a reluctant smile that told him she understood exactly what he meant. But to his regret, she didn't come back with a retort. She just changed the subject. She asked him what he'd been doing and he was happy to fill her in. Whether she was really interested or not, he didn't know. The important thing was that she was making an effort to think about something else. Maybe she was still thinking about the doctor who had hurt her so badly, but at least they weren't talking about him, and that had to be a good thing.

Another weekend approached. Amanda packed her overnight bag, but this time Nurse Whitmore wasn't available and her substitute wasn't interested in football, golf or anything much. She did her job, then disappeared into the spare room. The two days dragged by while Rahman tried to work but found himself thinking about Amanda instead, wondering what she was doing, imagining her out dancing with men who were strong and well and had goals and were good dancers too. Over and over he replayed their few moments of passion in his room. He had no idea if she was filled with regret or shame or if she'd forgotten it completely. He only knew he was filled with the most intense longing he'd ever known.

By Sunday afternoon he was counting the minutes until Amanda got back. But instead of hearing from Amanda, he got a call from Nicole, his friend from San Francisco. She'd been skiing all day and wanted to stop by and see him. He told her how to get to the house, told her the housekeeper was off so he couldn't invite her to dinner. She said not to worry, she couldn't stay long, and she'd bring some beer. He didn't want to tell her he couldn't drink any alcohol because of the medicines he was taking. It made him sound like a wimp and an invalid. But she'd see soon enough that he wasn't the same man she once knew. The man who was always on the go. From skiing in the morning in the Sierras to surfing the same afternoon in the ocean. He had to face the fact that he might never be that man again.

He hobbled to the front door to meet her and he could tell by the look on her face, Nicole hadn't realized the extent of his injuries. Or she had imagined he would have recovered by now. Her jaw dropped in surprise to see him gripping his walker as he led her to the living room. He saw her gaze lock onto the scar on his forehead, and knew she was noting the way he'd lost weight and couldn't walk without help. He'd gotten used to seeing himself in the mirror, but to her, the change in him must have been a shock.

"How are you, Rahman?" she asked, sitting across from him on the edge of a large couch in the great room. He had the feeling she was ready to bolt at a moment's notice. He got himself into a chair, gritting his teeth as sharp pain shot through his hip. He was trying to cut down on pain medicine, trying to tough it out. Maybe this wasn't a good time to have done so.

Nicole was watching him with wide eyes. "Can I… Is there anything I can do for you?"

"No, I'm much better, actually."

"Are you? I'm glad to hear it. Everyone's been so worried about you. I promised to report on your condition."

"Tell everyone I'm fine. I've gotten back to work..." He wasn't about to tell Nicole, as he'd told Amanda, that he'd never worked much before. There were things he'd told Amanda that he'd never told anyone and didn't intend to. "I should be able to come back to the city in a week or two."

"Really?" She looked surprised. "How have you managed up here by yourself?"

"Oh, I'm not by myself. I have a housekeeper and a full-time nurse. Both of whom are off today, but Amanda should be back soon." He didn't realize how often he'd been looking at his watch or glancing out the window waiting for her to arrive. Nicole was talking but he wasn't really listening to her. He was listening for the sound of the tires on the snow-packed driveway.

Finally he heard his car in the driveway. Amanda came in the front door, in a red, hooded ski jacket, her cheeks pink and her eyes bright. He didn't have to ask if she'd had a good weekend. She looked radiant. He wondered if she'd met that special man she'd described to him. He didn't know if he could bear it if she had.

He introduced the two women, then Amanda excused herself to go tell the replacement nurse she was back. Rahman watched her go, admiring the way her hips moved, and the way her hair brushed her shoulders. He forced himself to focus back on Nicole.

"Tell me about everybody back in the city. What's been happening?" he asked.

Nicole launched into a commentary on all the parties, the friends who attended them and the different activities

he'd missed. She told him who had paired off with
whom and which couples had split up. "Of course it's
not the same without you and Lisa," she said.

He nodded slowly.

"Sorry," she said. "I didn't mean to bring up Lisa.
Are you getting over it?" she asked.

"I'll never get over it," he said grimly. "I'll always
remember her."

Amanda paused in the doorway with a tray of soft
drinks and crackers. Neither Rahman nor his friend Nicole could see her. She shouldn't have been surprised to
hear that Rahman would always remember Lisa. He
must have loved her very much. He must still love her.
She shouldn't let it upset her, but she felt a sinking sen-
sation in the pit of her stomach.

She decided this wasn't the right time to intrude on
their conversation so she turned and walked back to the
kitchen. Clarice had left a ham studded with cloves and
covered with pineapple slices for their dinner which
Amanda slid into the oven, along with vegetables that
would roast along with the meat. There would be plenty
for his friend Nicole. Amanda would serve them in the
dining room and have a quiet dinner by herself in her
room.

She'd been thinking about having dinner with Rahman, telling him what she'd done and finding out how
he'd gotten along with the new nurse, but that wasn't
going to happen. The nurse had been relieved to see her.
To her, working this weekend had been just that—work.
She took no pleasure in it and apparently had had little
contact or conversation with her patient. A far cry from
Nurse Whitmore.

A few minutes later Nicole appeared in the kitchen.
She really was a very pretty girl with straight blond hair

and dazzling blue eyes. She wore diamond studs in her
ears and an expensive après-ski outfit. Just the kind of
woman Rahman would no doubt end up with. Someone
like him, accustomed to the good life, skiing at Tahoe
in the winter and summers at dude ranches or traveling
in Europe. She'd probably been a debutante who now
filled her time with volunteer work. They'd make a stunning couple.

Nicole had a worried frown on her face. "Can I ask
you something?" she said to Amanda after closing the
kitchen door behind her. "Is he going to get well?"

"Of course," Amanda said. "He's come a long way.
In a few weeks he'll have the tube out of his chest
and…"

"There's a tube in his chest?" she asked, her mouth
twisted in a grimace.

"Well, yes, to allow for the drainage. His lung collapsed, you know. Or maybe you didn't. Anyway the
tube is coming out soon. His lung is almost back to
normal. Of course it will take some time before his broken ribs have healed completely, but he's making incredible progress. He's very motivated."

Nicole's face paled. Maybe Amanda shouldn't have
explained in such detail. She tended to forget not everyone was interested in medicine, even if it concerned a
good friend.

"But will he ever be back to normal?" she asked.
"He used to hang glide and bungee jump."

"It's too soon to tell. I'd say he can probably do whatever he wants, eventually. But I don't know if he'll want
to take chances like that anymore. It's been a sobering
experience, as you might imagine. He might have hurt
himself much worse. He might even have killed himself
if he'd hit a tree head-on."

Nicole gave a little shudder. "So that's why Rahman's so…so sober, so serious. I guess you didn't know him before, before the accident. He was so much fun. At least, he was before Lisa died. He's not the same. I was wondering if he really would be himself again. The old Rahman I used to know. Never took anything too seriously. But now…"

"I guess a serious accident like that would change anyone," Amanda said. "But don't give up on him. He needs his friends. He's looking forward to returning to his old life. He's come a long way, not just physically, but mentally. His attitude has made a huge improvement—one hundred eighty degrees. The doctor's very pleased. So am I."

Nicole tilted her head to one side and observed Amanda carefully. "Are you?" she said at last as if she'd suddenly realized something important. Then without waiting for an answer, she said she'd have to be going. Amanda invited her to stay for dinner, but she said she couldn't. She went back to the living room and kissed Rahman goodbye, murmuring something Amanda couldn't hear, and walked out the door.

Amanda found his medicine, filled a cup with water and then waited for a few minutes to give Rahman a chance to pull himself together. She had no idea what his feelings were for this woman. Even though she'd heard him say he'd never forget Lisa, that didn't mean he wouldn't fall in love again, and Nicole might be the one. She was the only one to visit him since his stay in the hospital. That must mean something.

While Amanda was standing in the shadow of the hallway, Rahman called her. "Amanda? Where are you? What are you doing?" he called hoarsely. Then when he saw her, he said, "It's about time."

"I thought you were busy with your friend, so I..."

"I've had the worst weekend."

"Oh, no," she said sympathetically, handing him four small pills and the cup of water. "I gather this nurse wasn't exactly as much fun as Dorothy Whitmore."

He tossed the pills down, gulped the water and then shook his head. "I'm not asking that she entertain me. But is it too much to ask that she at least smile occasionally or say something pleasant? I guess I can't blame her. I'm not the easiest patient in the world, am I?"

Amanda stood in the middle of the room looking at him. He might not be the easiest patient, but he was by far the most attractive she'd ever had, and the most interesting and the most challenging. That was her opinion, but maybe she was biased. She wished she weren't. She wished he was just another patient. She wished she could view him more clearly. But her vision was clouded with a large helping of emotion. She only hoped no one else guessed how she felt about him. Especially not Rahman.

"Never mind," he said, when he saw her trying to formulate an answer. "Sit down and tell me about your weekend."

She sat down and tucked her legs up underneath her. "I took a skiing lesson."

"What?"

"Yes, Rosie's girls were enrolled in ski class and I was watching them come down the hill behind their instructor. I watched them fall down and get right up again and it looked like so much fun I got into an adult class."

"How did you do? Did you like it? Did you fall?" The words tumbled out like the water rushing over the stones in the Truckee River.

She had to laugh at his nonstop interrogation.

"Yes, I fell. Yes, I liked it. I guess I did all right. I went down the bunny slope about a dozen times. I must have looked awful. The instructor kept yelling at me to bend my knees and turn my skis into the hill. Easy for him to say. And easy for him to do. If only I'd started about twenty years ago."

"You're not giving up, are you?" he asked. "Skiing is the greatest. Wait till you get up there on top of the mountain...there's nothing like shussing down from the top."

"Oh, it'll be a while before I get up there," she said. "A long while. But no, I'm not giving up. I'm scheduled for another lesson next weekend."

He drew his eyebrows together. "I wish I could be there to coach you. Are you sure this instructor is any good?"

"He seems fine. Very patient. But how do I know? How good does he have to be to teach a beginner like me?" she asked.

"As long as you... As long as he... Oh, damn, I wish I was well." Rahman punched his fist into a cushion. Beginning skiers were always falling for their ski instructors who were invariably tall and blond and tanned and called Hans or Ivor. Amanda was so vulnerable. She might be susceptible to one of them hitting on her in the bar afterward over a hot buttered rum.

"Nicole wishes you were well, too. I'm sorry she couldn't stay for dinner."

"I'm not," he said. "I can't imagine what we would have talked about. She's the most vapid, uninteresting—" He broke off. "So, what else did you do? Did you go to any of those après-ski bars?"

"Just one. Just to warm up."

Just one. That's all it took. "Did anyone hit on you?" he asked.

"What kind of a question is that?" she asked. "I talked to some people. Everyone's so friendly."

"I'll bet," he said with stiff lips. He knew what those bar scenes were like. Everyone looking everyone over, sizing up the good-looking women. That's what he used to do. If he'd seen Amanda there, he wouldn't have hesitated to approach her and try out one of his many lines. What would she have done? Did she know how to get rid of the men who were annoying her? Or weren't they annoying her? She probably enjoyed talking about her day on the slopes with them. He could hear it now.

"*Good day?*"

"*Not bad. I took a few falls.*"

"*Where are you from?*"

"*Chicago.*"

"*Chicago? You came all this way to ski at Squaw Valley?*"

And so it would go until Amanda had agreed to join some macho hot-dogger for a drink. Rahman's eyes narrowed, he felt more frustrated than before. She didn't seem to notice anything was wrong.

"If you're okay, I might run off and have a hot bath. It was cold up there on those slopes." She shivered, stood and rubbed her hip.

"What's wrong?" he asked. "Did you hurt yourself?"

"I took a few falls, nothing serious. Just a bruise."

"Let me see," he demanded.

She shot him a look of surprise.

"Come on," he said. "There's no room for modesty between you and me. You've seen most all of me at my worst. Do I get embarrassed? No. I just want to make sure you didn't hurt yourself. I've heard medical people are the last ones to admit they're injured."

"That's just a rumor," she said. But she walked over to him and pulled her waistband down an inch or two and he got a look at an ugly black bruise on her hip. "See, it's nothing." she said.

He ran his hand gently over the bruised skin and she shivered again. He wanted to run his hands over both hips. He wanted to reach up under her sweater and cup her breasts in his palms.

"Go," he said gruffly. "Go take your bath." He sat there watching the dusk fall over the snow-covered mountains. He couldn't hear the water running in her bathroom at the end of the hall, but he could imagine her taking her clothes off. He knew what she'd look like as the steam filled the room. She'd be Venus on the half shell. Slim hips, long legs, flat stomach and full breasts. He felt a wave of desire wash over him so strong he thought he might be hyperventilating.

That's all he needed, on top of everything else. She'd come back and find him passed out on the couch. An overdose of Amanda without every having made love to her, or even trying. Or even told her how he felt about her. That she was the sweetest, kindest, loveliest woman he'd ever met. That he was only sorry they'd met under such adverse circumstances. That if he ever loved again or cared again, it would certainly be someone like her.

Someone like her? There was no one like her. He knew that with a certainty that shook him to the soles of his feet. She was one of a kind, but she was only his nurse. No doubt every patient she'd ever had felt that way about her. He was just one in a list of many. And there'd be many more. The thought of her taking care of other men, bathing them, massaging their muscles, giving them their medicine, telling them the story of her life made him feel sick and so lonely he ached all over.

When he left the house and went back to the city he'd be left with only his memories. There were those kisses that day in his room which she was quick to apologize for. He was sorry, too. But for different reasons. He was sorry they'd stopped so soon. Sorry they hadn't really talked about it, about what it meant. But he was afraid to learn what he suspected, that the only feelings she had for him were those of sympathy.

She came back to the living room smelling of shampoo and soap and positively glowing.

"You look…great," he said, trying to keep his voice even. "Skiing agrees with you. How do you feel?"

"Tired, hungry. What about you?"

"Better, now that you're here. And more determined to get out of here as soon as possible."

She nodded soberly. "It won't be long now. When Heidi comes tomorrow we should ask her about continuing your therapy in the city. Whether you should get your own equipment or go into a rehab center as an outpatient."

"I wouldn't have enough room in my apartment for all the apparatus I have here."

"You have an apartment? I thought maybe…"

"Maybe I lived with my family? No. I have a place on Russian Hill in a high-rise with a view of the bay and the bridge. It's quite spectacular. You'll have to come and see it."

She nodded, but she didn't look the least bit interested in seeing his apartment. Why should she? When he left there, their relationship would be over.

"I'll miss you," he said. He didn't mean to say it.

Not now. It wasn't appropriate, but he couldn't help it. He couldn't imagine life without her.

"I'll miss you, too," she said. But there was no emotion, no warmth in her voice. She was just being polite and it hurt. "But once you get back to your old life you'll hardly remember this episode. It will just be a blip in your memory. You'll have so much to do, so much to think about, so many people to see who will be glad to see you back."

"I'm not going back to my old life," he said. It was true. His old life of parties and nonstop fun and empty-headed friends no longer appealed to him. He had goals now, goals to make his family proud of him. He'd like to make Amanda proud of him too, but would they keep in touch, would he ever see her again?

"That will make things even better," she said. "Make the transition easier for you."

"You think so?" he asked.

"I'm sure of it. You've switched your focus. You have a whole new outlook on life. That happens to people when they've been through what you've been through. The lucky ones anyway."

"I've been lucky," he said. "Very lucky. Lucky to have found you. No, it wasn't luck. It was fate. Fate brought us together."

"I think it was Rosie's Home Health Service," she said. "If it hadn't been me, it would have been someone else. You still would have gotten well."

"My body would have recovered I suppose. But not my mind. I see things differently and that's because of you."

"It that's true, then I'm glad. I must admit I've changed too since I first arrived here. I feel much better about myself and life in general."

"No desire to go back to Chicago?"

"None at all. But I'm able to look back without the anger and the bitterness I came with."

"Dorothy Whitmore says it's time that heals and then it's keeping busy. At least that's how she got over her loss."

"She's a wise woman," Amanda said.

Rahman noticed she gave no credit to him for helping her getting over her former love. That was because he didn't deserve any. He owed her, but she didn't owe him anything.

Chapter Eight

After that evening things moved so fast Amanda felt someone had pushed the fast forward switch to speed up her life. In the following two weeks, Rahman got permission from the doctor and the therapist to relocate to the city. He'd made progress not only in getting well, but in his business. He looked better, he had more energy and he put his energy to good use, both mentally and physically. But when he got the news he didn't look as ecstatic as she thought he would. After all, it was all he'd wanted, since the first moment she'd met him—to get back to San Francisco and his old life. Instead of jumping with joy, which wasn't possible given the condition of his weak ankle, he smiled with satisfaction, but looked pensive.

In his bedroom which was more office these days than anything else, he told her about some small businesses he was going to fund, about some investments he was investigating and shared his excitement with her about the possibilities. She couldn't believe the change in him.

He still couldn't put much weight on his ankle, he still got tired in the afternoons, he still had pains in his chest, but his eyes were bright and his high cheekbones were was tinged with color as he talked about the ventures he was going to invest in.

She knew she was only in the loop because he hadn't told his father or brother what he was doing. Not yet. She was the only one around he had to confide in. Once he was back at the office in the city, he'd take his place where he'd always belonged, but never fit in before, as a full partner. He'd go to meetings and conferences and he'd never miss her.

"That portrait of your grandfather, you told me about," she said to him one afternoon. "I imagine he'll still be looking down at you when you come into the office, but now he'll be looking at you in a new way, with pride and approval." When that happened, he'd know he'd turned his life around. He'd never need her again, not to confide in, not to take care of him, not for anything. In fact, she'd most likely never hear from him again. But she wouldn't forget him. She'd be happy for him. Happy and proud of him for what he'd done on his own.

"I hope so," he said. "I'm going to do my best. I only hope it's good enough. I've got years to make up for."

The day before he left, Amanda was packing her bags. She looked around the room at the tasteful furnishings, at the room that had been her home these past weeks and realized how far she'd come. Not just in miles from Chicago, but in leaving behind a chapter in her life. She could truly say she no longer thought of the emergency room back at St. Vincent's with dread and shame. She remembered the good times, the camaraderie with the other nurses, the orderlies and the med-techs. The thrill of saving lives, the split-second decisions. It had been an exciting time but it was over. She'd made a big mistake and she'd paid the price. Now that she was over it, what was next?

She gazed out at the view of the snow-covered mountains she would never tire of looking at and sighed. How she'd miss this house. How much more she'd miss the owner. They'd shared so much. So many ups and downs. When Rahman came to the door, she turned around and stared at him as if to memorize his face. As if she'd ever forget it. She couldn't believe she would never see him again after tomorrow. She also couldn't believe she'd let herself get emotionally involved with a patient. She thought she'd learned a lesson back in Chicago. Yes, she'd gotten over her infatuation with Ben. But how to get over the cure? She only knew she had to get over it, and she would, even if it took years.

"Tell me again where you're going," he said, surveying her open suitcase with a frown.

"To rent a room from a friend of Rosie's," she said, forcing herself to smile cheerfully. "I'll have my own bath and a private entrance. Of course there's no view like this one, but it's really very nice. And so is Jenny, her friend."

"Couldn't Rosie find you another private duty job?"

"Of course, but that's not what I want."

"I don't blame you. An experience like this must have turned you against private duty for good."

She smiled at his effort at levity. "You know that's not true. I've loved every minute of it."

"Every minute?" He raised his eyebrows.

"Well, almost." She didn't know if he was referring to the kiss or his bursts of temper. In any case, they were all best forgotten. "I think I'll give the hospital a try. They're desperate for RNs to work the night shift."

"That sounds dismal."

She stiffened. Whatever he felt for her, she didn't want pity. "To you, maybe. But it doesn't have to be. It can be fulfilling to care for people in the middle of the night when they're at their lowest and need someone. Then I'll have my days free."

"Free for what?" he asked.

"Whatever I want. I bought a ski pass. I intend to continue my lessons."

"I wish I could have skied with you," he said. "I hope someday…"

He didn't finish his sentence. He must realize that that skiing together wasn't possible. It wasn't only that he wasn't ready to ski yet or that she'd never be at his level once he'd recovered. It was that their paths would never cross again.

The next day, the limo his family sent from San Francisco came to pick him up before she left. They stood together at the front door in the cold windy air huddled in the doorway while they watched the long black car pull up to the front of the house. She tried to think of something to say but she couldn't. She couldn't say what was in her heart and anything else sounded empty and meaningless. The fir trees that flanked the house were heavy with snow. The skies were gray and overcast. Rosie had gotten delayed in picking her up. It was a strange feeling to be the last one to leave. As if she belonged there and he didn't.

She walked with him down the steps to where the chauffeur was waiting. She was afraid Rahman might slip on the icy walkway because of his stiff ankle, but she didn't want to take his arm because he was convinced he was back to normal and would have rejected her help. The driver opened the door and Rahman turned and put his hands firmly on her shoulders. He looked deep into her eyes, his gaze so intense she was shaking inside and out.

"When will I see you again?" he asked.

"I...I'm not sure," she said, trying to avoid his gaze, but unable to tear her eyes away. She couldn't say never. It was too painful, but it was the truth. She bit her lip to keep it from trembling.

"What about that conference you're coming to in San Francisco?"

She was hoping he'd forgotten about that. "Oh, that. I'm not sure I'll be able to go. It depends on my schedule."

"If you come, call me. Here's my card." He reached into his pocket and pulled out a business card. "If I'm not at the office, you can always get me on my cell phone. I'd like to show you around. It's the least I can do after all you've done for me."

She stuffed the card into her pocket. She wanted to protest that all she'd done for him was what any nurse would have done. But that would only prolong this conversation that she wished would be over. She shifted from one foot to the other. Why didn't he get in the car and go? The chauffeur was standing at a discreet distance, waiting politely.

"If not, I'll see you back here. I'll be coming back to the house, maybe I'll even be back on skis one of these days. We could take a run together," he said.

"That would be nice," she said. She hated to hear herself sound so cool and polite, as if she barely knew him. But it was better than bursting into tears. It was better than throwing her arms around him and begging

him not to go. His forehead was creased into a frown.
If he didn't leave soon she didn't think she could control
herself much longer. She blinked back the tears in her
eyes.

"It's the wind," she murmured, brushing the back of
her gloved hand across her face.

"You'd better get back inside," he said. Then he
leaned down and kissed her. She wasn't expecting it. A
brief goodbye kiss, maybe. But this was a kiss that was
full of passion and longing and regret. A moment ago
she'd been shaking with cold and fear that he'd guess
what she was feeling. Now she was burning up.

She didn't care if he guessed what she was feeling.
She was no longer capable of hiding her feelings. She
kissed him with a hunger she'd been denying existed. She
kissed him with a fervor she couldn't stifle. Despite
the wind and the cold she felt like she was on fire. His
fingers dug into the soft wool of her jacket. She wrapped
herself around him so tightly he couldn't leave even if
he'd wanted to.

She was vaguely aware of a blue jay screeching from
the branch of a fir tree. He was probably telling her to
let go, let Rahman get on his way, back to his real life
and for her to get back in the house. But she blocked
out the warnings. She blocked out everything but the
desperate needs that tore through her body. Needs she'd
denied for too long. The need to be loved, the need to
belong to someone, to be cherished, to be taken care of.
For so long she'd taken care of everyone else.

She'd denied the passion she felt every time she
touched Rahman or exchanged a heated glance. For once
she let herself go. Everything she'd held back came rushing out in a torrent of forbidden ecstasy. It felt so good
to be in his arms, so right, so safe, so thrilling.

She kissed him again and again, oblivious to the wind and the cold, to the chauffeur, to the blue jay. Conscious only of the heat from his body, the strength he'd regained, the force of his will. They were on equal ground there for just a moment. Just him and her and the chauffeur and the blue jay. No longer nurse and patient. Just man and woman. A man who'd been grieving a lost love. A woman who'd been betrayed. All that was forgotten. But not for long.

The moment was over when it started to snow. They broke apart and looked up at the sky. It was better to look anywhere than at each other. Wet flakes swirled around them. He looked down at her and brushed a snowflake from her cheek with infinite tenderness. Tenderness she didn't expect from him. Tears sprang to her eyes once again.

"Goodbye," he said. And then he was gone. She stood in front of the house as the snow came faster and thicker until she couldn't see his car anymore. Then she ran into the house, sank into the couch in the living room and burst into tears. She wasn't sure why she was crying. Was it because she'd never see him again? Was it because she regretted not telling him how she felt about him? Or was it because a chapter in her life was over and she was starting over again? The house seemed cold and empty without him. It wasn't cold, it was warm and snug. It wasn't empty, either, Clarice was somewhere, probably in the kitchen. She'd said her goodbye earlier.

Amanda wiped her eyes. How many times would she go through this? How many times would she fall in love with someone she couldn't have? How many times would her heart be broken? Would she ever learn?

Amanda was right about one thing, Rahman thought as he walked into the office two weeks later. His grandfather's face in the portrait no longer frowned at him. Nobody in the office frowned at him. They simply stared in amazement as he returned to work. Every time he stayed late, or called a meeting, or came up with a fresh idea, he could see the meaningful glances, the smiles, and the knowing looks. As if he'd taken time out for a personality transplant, an infusion of the work ethic instead of therapy for a punctured lung and a broken ankle.

They used the words "return to work" when Rahman knew they weren't appropriate. Of course it was nice to be appreciated, but he couldn't help wondering just how bad he'd been before the accident. He was blessed with a kind of amnesia of those days. Maybe because he didn't want to remember the kind of man he was then. He leafed backward through his desk calendar and there it was in black and white. His appointments on a typical day told the tale.

Golf 9:00 a.m.

Lunch with Liz at Green's. 12:00

Handball at the club. 4:00

Cocktails with Lisa at Emmenthal's. 6:00 p.m.

Party at J's

And so it went.

The sight of Lisa's name scattered all through his calendar gave him a chill. She'd always be part of his past. A bright star in his memory. He'd never forget the good times they'd had. But he no longer grieved or felt bitter about her death. He didn't see much of the old crowd. He didn't have time to party anymore, nor did he miss it.

When his brother dropped by his office, he had a few questions for him.

"I was pretty bad, wasn't I?"

"How do you mean?"

He flipped the pages of the calendar. "I mean I never did any work, did I?"

"Not much." Rafik sat on the edge of Rahman's desk. "I hate to say this, but if it hadn't been for that accident…"

"I'd still be a bum, is that what you were going to say?"

Rafik shrugged. He didn't need to say it. "What happened? When we left you at the house you were a mess. You had this attitude that fate had dealt you a blow. Physically and mentally. That must have been some nurse we left you with. What she did was a miracle."

Rahman didn't say anything. He looked out the window at the view of the city skyscrapers and the dark blue San Francisco Bay in the distance. He'd tried not to think of Amanda. Tried not to imagine her getting back to a normal life. Working nights, skiing during the day, hitting the after ski spots, going to dances, meeting strange men. She'd been decidedly cool when he suggested meeting again. He'd gotten the message that to her he was just another patient. That now that he was well, there was no need for them to see each other again. But that didn't stop him from thinking about her, remembering their conversations.

And then there was that kiss. That goodbye kiss in the snow. That was the only thing that kept him from falling into despair. The heat from her body, the passion of the kiss kept him wondering, hoping… Did she care more than she let on? What if…

For the first time in his life he found work challenging. He had the satisfaction of taking his place in the family business after all these years. His father and his brother both appreciated his new attitude toward work

Those were good things. But there was a hole in his life. There was a pain behind the cracked ribs that was located in his heart.

He missed her. He missed her smile, the healing touch of her hands that both cooled and heated his skin, her voice urging him forward on the parallel bars, faster on the training stairs. Her voice—the last thing he heard at night and the first thing in the morning. There was the way she listened to him, no matter what nonsense he was talking. No matter how much he complained or demanded. She was always there. Of course it was her job. He was probably listening to someone else now. He'd probably meant no more to her than any other patient.

On the other hand, there was that kiss... His lips curved in a smile just thinking about it. How many times had he relived it, wishing he'd taken it to another level, gone back in the house, talked about it...analyzed it... Kissed her again to make sure he wasn't imagining her rapid heartbeat that matched his own, her flushed cheeks, her tear-filled eyes.

"Rahman?" His brother waved his hand in front of his face. "Is there something you haven't told me? What happened there in the mountains?"

"Nothing." Rahman forced himself back to the present. "I got some great care, great therapy and I worked hard at it. No miracles involved. Just a lot of hard work."

"What about the nurse, what was her name?"

"Amanda." He didn't mean it, but his voice caught and her name came out in a half whisper.

"Anything happen between you?"

"Of course not," Rahman said indignantly. Maybe too forcefully. His brother gave him a sharp glance.

"She's a professional. Even if I'd wanted to. I was in no condition to...to...it would have been..." He was stumbling for the right word. It would have been wrong, of course it would have been wrong. But it would have been heaven to make love to Amanda.

"I understand," Rafik said. "I'm not blind, you know. You fell in love with your nurse."

"Don't be ridiculous," Rahman exclaimed. "I may have been infatuated with her..."

"It's not unusual to fall in love with a nurse," Rafik said. "She was nice looking as I recall."

"Nice looking? She was beautiful."

"With a pleasant personality."

"Pleasant? Don't talk about things you know nothing about. You didn't know her. You didn't spend weeks with her. You don't know the story of her life. You don't know what she's been through." He bit his tongue to keep from saying, *You don't know how she looks in the morning before she has her coffee. You don't know how warm her lips are in the middle of a snowstorm, you don't know how much I miss her, how much I love her...* He stopped suddenly. He didn't know where he'd gotten the idea that he loved her. But once it was there in his mind he couldn't get rid of it. Was that what love was? That ache in his heart, that constant longing for someone and something you couldn't have? How should he know? Rafik would know.

"No, I don't know anything about her," Rafik said soberly. "But if I were you, I wouldn't let her get away."

"Oh, really," Rahman said. "For your information she has gotten away. She's up at Tahoe and I'm here. She has a job there I have a job here." He sat down in his office chair and looked at his brother. "When you met Anne, how did you know she was the one? I mean how did you know you were in love?''

Rafik gazed out the window for a long moment. The sounds of the city streets below were muted. ''I couldn't stop thinking about her. I'd never felt lonely before, but the prospect of spending my life without her was intolerable. Is that love? You tell me. I only know if it isn't, it will have to do until the real thing comes along.''

Rahman gave him a wry smile. ''You're lucky,'' he murmured.

''I know.'' Phones were ringing elsewhere, there were footsteps in the hall but in Rahman's office there was silence. ''Can't you go up there and see her?'' Rafik said.

''No, I can't,'' Rahman said brusquely. He didn't want to tell his brother that Amanda didn't want to see him. She'd made it quite clear she'd be too busy. In other words, she wasn't interested.

''Then maybe she'll come to the city. She can't stay in the mountains forever, can she? She'll need a break some time. She can't work every day.''

''She is coming to the city, for a nursing conference, but...'' But he didn't know when and he was afraid she wouldn't call him when she came. She'd taken his card and put it in her pocket without looking at it as if she had to get rid of it quickly. It might be contaminated with some kind of virus. No, she wasn't going to call him. Why? Had he been that obnoxious? Was it part of the Hippocratic oath that nurses took that forbade them from ever fraternizing with ex-patients? ''I don't know when it is.''

''Find out,'' his brother said. He looked at his watch. ''I have to go. I'm meeting Anne for lunch. Let me know what happens.''

"Nothing will happen," Rahman said, but Rafik didn't hear him, he was already out the door and into the hall.

It wasn't that hard to find out when the conference was and where it was being held. What he didn't know was if Amanda was coming to it. He didn't know how to get in touch with her and didn't know what to say even if he did. He decided to go to the convention hotel and see if she was registered.

The clerk at the desk told him he couldn't say whether she was registered or not. Security reasons.

Rahman turned abruptly from the front desk and scanned the crowd. Before the accident, he would have insisted the clerk tell him. He would have called the manager and pulled rank. Now he only strode across the lobby that was full of women and a handful of men all wearing name tags. He heard snatches of conversation.

"Working ten-hour-shifts…"

"High turnover but that doesn't mean…"

"I didn't go into nursing to fill out forms all day."

"Have you seen Cindy? She's going back to school."

Where was Amanda? Was this a national convention? Would Amanda see her old friends from Chicago? Would they tell her how much they missed her and how much a certain doctor missed her?

Would she decide to go back? Was she still in love with that scoundrel? He stopped next to a small group of conventioneers and asked if any of them had seen Amanda Reston.

"Who?"

They shook their heads. Didn't know her. Hadn't seen her. He sat down in the lounge on the mezzanine that overlooked the lobby and ordered coffee. That way he could watch the crowd without looking out of place.

He drummed his fingers on the table and kept watching. He began to feel ridiculous. Sitting there waiting for someone who might be two hundred miles away. Or even across the street or having a drink at the top of the Mark Hopkins. A group of nurses sat down at the table next to his and he eavesdropped shamelessly. He heard all about their problems with salary and bosses and schedules but he didn't hear anything about Amanda. When they left, he picked up a schedule of events they'd left on the table.

He noticed workshops on treating the mentally ill, workshops on dealing with parents of sick children, but he had no idea which ones she'd go to or if he'd be allowed in to any of them. When he looked up, he saw her at the far end of the lobby. He jumped up, threw down some money on the table and edged his way across the floor.

"Excuse me. Pardon me. I'm sorry," he said as he inched his way toward her. It was maddening how many people were in his way.

"Amanda," he shouted. His voice was lost in the general din. She didn't turn around. When he finally reached her she was about to enter the revolving door on her way out. He went in with her and tapped her on the shoulder. She turned and a strange woman looked at him with a puzzled frown.

"Sorry," he said, his face turning dull red. "I thought you were someone else."

The woman raised her eyebrows and rushed out into the street, probably assuming he was some kind of nut.

"Damn," he muttered to himself. "Damn, damn, damn." He stood there on the sidewalk, watching the people go in and out of the hotel. He didn't see Amanda, but he saw her friend Rosie come through the door. She recognized him and said hello.

"Where's Amanda?" he asked as soon as he'd murmured a few pleasantries. "Did she come?"

"Yes, of course she came. I thought you knew she'd be here. I think she might be changing her clothes in the room," she said. "She's going out to dinner with some of her old friends from nursing school. This is an incredible conference, getting caught up on the latest trends in nursing as well as old friends. We've had a really busy day. I'm on my way to a meeting right now."

"Do you think I could see her?" Rahman asked.

Rosie hesitated only a moment. "Sure. Why not? It's room 1572. Maybe you should call her on the house phone first to make sure she's there."

He nodded, thanked her and headed for one of the white phones. His head was pounding. He'd come to see her but now that he knew where she was, he was afraid of finding out once again that she had no desire to see him. Maybe he shouldn't call first. It would just give her a chance to say no. Maybe if he was on the other side of the door, she'd feel sorry for him and let him in.

He took the elevator to the fifteenth floor. When he found her room, he stood there with his hand clenched in a fist, ready to knock, for a long moment. He thought he heard voices. Maybe he should leave, go down to the lobby and call her after all. No. He had to see her, face-to-face, to find out if she was totally indifferent to him or if there was a chance she felt anything at all for him. If she'd give him the chance to show her he'd changed. Maybe he hadn't changed enough. He remembered what she said she was looking for—a man who knew what he wanted and how to get it. He knew what he wanted. He wanted her. But he didn't know how to get her.

"Yes?"

"Amanda, it's Rahman."

She opened the door wearing a dark-wine colored wool dress and high heels. Her hair was pulled behind her ears and gold hoops dangled from her ears. He stared and swallowed hard trying to catch his breath. He felt like he'd run up the fifteen floors instead of taking the elevator. On the other hand, she looked completely calm and composed. She didn't even look that surprised to see him. Had she been expecting him? Why hadn't she called him? His heart pounded deep in his chest. He braced his arms on the door frame in case his legs gave way.

"Rahman, what are you doing here?"

"I came to see you. I thought you'd call, but you didn't."

"I was going to, but…"

She didn't finish her sentence. How could she? She had no excuse for not calling him. She simply didn't want to see him again. He wondered if she'd even ask him to come in. From the euphoria to seeing her again to the despair of realizing she didn't care had him reeling.

"How are you?" she asked.

"Fine. Great." He didn't feel fine. He didn't feel great. He felt like he'd been punched in the stomach.

"I'm on my way out," she said. "Why don't you come in for a minute and meet an old friend of mine?"

"A friend from nursing school?"

"Yes, how did you know?"

She stood back and he walked into the room. There stood a tall, muscular man in a suit and tie.

"Rob Anderson," the man said, holding out his hand.

Rahman muttered his name and shook hands with the man. This was her nurse friend? Of course he knew men could be nurses, but somehow it hadn't occurred to him her friend would be a man, definitely not a man who looked more like a football player than a nurse. Rahman stood there staring at him while he and Amanda explained how they'd run into each other after all these years since graduation and so on. Rahman hardly knew what they were saying. All he could think of was that Amanda was going out with another man. Here in his city. Out on the town where he'd planned to take her. Out without him.

He switched his gaze from her to her friend Rob and back again. They obviously had a lot in common. A lot to talk about. She might even tell Rob about himself and what a difficult patient he'd been. He felt a dull ache in the back of his head.

"We really ought to go," Rob said. "We're meeting the gang at Mings Restaurant at eight."

Mings! The famous Chinese restaurant on the wharf. Rahman had wanted to take her there. He knew exactly what he'd order—the Peking duck and the famous pork cooked in a clay pot. Out-of-towners wouldn't know about that.

"Would you care to join us?" Rob asked.

Rob asked. Not Amanda. She looked surprised and not especially pleased.

"No, thanks," Rahman said. He could imagine himself at the far end of the table of nurses, separated from Amanda by acres of strange faces. The conversation peppered with in-terms he wouldn't understand.

Amanda looked relieved.

"What about tomorrow night?" Rahman asked Amanda. "Are you free for dinner?"

"Well, I…"

"Oh, wait a minute," he said. "Tomorrow night is my parents' anniversary. We're having a family party. Would you, I mean would you consider going with me?"

"I wouldn't want to intrude," she said. She looked as if she wouldn't want to do anything with him. But he couldn't take no for an answer. It might be his only chance. If he let he get away, he didn't know what he'd do. He had to show her he'd changed. He had to prove to her he was the man she was looking for. Yes, it would take more than one evening, but it was a start.

"You wouldn't be intruding," he said. "My family wants a chance to thank you for all you've done for me." He turned to Rob, aware that he was being left out of the conversation. "Amanda was my private duty nurse when I fell down a mountain skiing."

"Yes, I know. She told me about that."

Rahman grated his back teeth together in frustration. So she had told this guy about him. Heaven only knew what she'd said. He was rich, arrogant and spoiled. And that was only for starters.

Amanda appeared to be wavering, looking at him with indecision written on her face. He had to think of something, anything.

"You owe me, you know," he said. She looked puzzled. "That Japanese dinner you never brought me. Remember?"

"Yes, but…"

"I'll pick you up here at seven."

She shrugged. At least she didn't flat turn him down. He decided to leave before she did.

"Nice meeting you, Rob," he said and left the room.

Chapter Nine

The next night when Rahman came to pick Amanda up she was waiting in the lobby. He heaved a sigh of relief. He was half afraid she wouldn't be there. He could imagine finding a note at the front desk containing some excuse. He didn't blame her for trying to avoid him. He was just one of her many past patients. He knew she felt differently about him than the others. But how much, he didn't know.

He wondered if she'd come down to the lobby because she didn't want to be alone with him in an intimate setting such as her room, though it didn't seem to bother her having Rob in her room. Whatever her reason, it didn't spoil his pleasure in seeing her again in the dark red dress that made her eyes sparkle and her cheeks glow.

"Forgive me for staring," he said. "But you look so different from the last time I saw you."

"But I'm wearing the same dress," she said with a smile.

"I meant back at the cabin," he said. "You know you ought to do that more often."

"What, wear the same dress?"

"No, smile."

Something flickered in her eyes, telling him they were sharing the same thought, the memory of the other times he'd said that same thing. He smiled back at her. They stood there in the middle of the lobby, with bellboys pushing luggage carts across the Oriental carpet, guests being paged, lines of people waiting to check in, but he didn't see or hear anything but her. He didn't know what she was thinking, but her gaze held his and didn't waver. He felt the strength of the connection between them, a bond that was there the first time he'd seen her in his hospital room and had never completely disappeared. He concentrated on sending her all the messages he'd stored up from the weeks they'd been apart. Words he wanted to say but didn't dare. Not now. Not here.

I love you.

I need you.

I don't want to live any longer without you.

Did she know? Did she hear? Did she care?

Finally, when he couldn't stand the suspense any longer, he took by the arm and led her outside to his waiting car.

Amanda hadn't wanted to see Rahman. She thought she'd be safe if she didn't call him. She hadn't counted on him coming to the hotel. She was having a hard enough time forgetting him without refreshing her memory of how handsome, how sexy, and how charming he was. She'd told herself he was not only handsome, sexy and charming, but he was arrogant, impossible, difficult, spoiled and on and on. Tonight he seemed to have none of these negative traits. Of course he was not sick any-more. Yes, she noticed he limped slightly, but other than that he exuded health and energy and so much more, she felt vibrations in the air just being with him.

"How do you feel?" she asked him in the comfort of the heated, leather seat of his luxury sedan.

"Fine. My doctor here is very impressed with the pro-gress I've made. Of course I still have a few problems, I'm still on some medication, but they say I'll be back to normal one of these days. Whatever that is. No one can believe that this is normal for me."

"What do you mean?"

"Working a lot. Playing very little."

"Sounds like you've turned your life around," she said, glancing at his profile, noticing the angle of his jaw, the stubborn chin, remembering how his lips felt on hers the day he said goodbye. It was a kiss she'd never forget, no matter how hard she tried. And she had tried. But the memory kept coming back. His arms around her, the passion that built and built and threatened to over-whelm her. The empty hole in her life when he was gone. The regrets. The things she could have said. Things she could have done. It was too late now. He had a new life and so did she. He had his old friends back and she had a few new ones.

She caught a hint of his shaving lotion, the same one he'd used at the cabin. The smell brought the memories rushing back and made her weak with longing. Longing to live under the same roof again, longing to be part of his life again, longing to see him the first thing every morning before he'd combed his hair or gotten out of bed and every evening in front of the fire. She told her-self to get over it. If he could turn his life around, so could she. She could stop living in the past, thinking about the weeks they'd spent under the same roof and get on with her life.

She turned back to look out at the traffic and crossed her arms over her waist. She told herself she'd have to stop fantasizing. Yes, he'd changed. Yes, he'd asked her to a family party. But to be realistic, he would have asked Nurse Whitmore if she'd been there, just as a courtesy and because he genuinely liked her. And she liked him.

"I saw Dorothy Whitmore the other day," Amanda said. "She was very touched by your generous gift."

"Yes, she sent me a nice thank-you note. How's she doing?"

"Fine. Especially now that she has that big screen TV. She invites all her neighbors in to watch the games on the weekends." Dorothy Whitmore liked Rahman before he'd sent her the giant TV, now she adored him. Couldn't say enough about his good nature, his generosity, his good looks. According to her, he must be the most eligible bachelor in California if not the world. She dared Amanda to disagree. Amanda didn't, not out loud anyway.

He smiled. "I would have sent you something too, but I didn't know what you wanted. What do you want?" he asked, turning to look at her.

Again his gaze caught hers and made it impossible to look away. She couldn't speak. Her mouth was dry. What could she say? You. I want you. Not an expensive gift, no matter how thoughtful. Not your money. Not your high-rise apartment or your luxurious ski house. Just you.

"Nothing," she said at last.

He nodded and turned his attention back to the road. "I thought that's what you'd say."

The anniversary party was held at his cousin Tarik's house on a bluff overlooking the sea. It was too dark to appreciate the view, but Amanda immediately felt the warmth and comfort of the interior which matched the warmth of the family's welcome. She was greeted enthusiastically by Rahman's twin brother, his wife and Rahman's parents. She met Carolyn, Tarik's wife and Yasmine, his younger sister.

Rahman's mother hugged her. Amanda felt a surge of emotion that almost choked her when the small woman put her arms around her. She felt a longing for her own mother, the loss that had left a gap in her life that had never been filled. The loss that she'd suppressed all these years made tears spring to her eyes. It made her realize all the special occasions, the celebrations, the birthdays and the anniversaries she'd missed. How lucky these people were to have each other.

His mother didn't appear to notice her momentary lack of composure. "We can't thank you enough for everything you've done for Rahman," she said.

"I didn't really do anything except what any nurse would have done," she said, collecting herself.

"Amanda is too modest, Mother," Rahman said. "She often performed over and above the duties of the average nurse. Before I met Amanda I had no idea how skilled nurses were in so many areas. You'd be amazed at the level of their ability. Not just giving medicine or injections. It goes far beyond that. They have to inspire and encourage the patients to get well. That includes more than what is in the nurse's manual. They'll do whatever it takes, won't you, Amanda?" he asked. His face was a mask of innocence, but the look in his eyes told her there was an underlying meaning to his words that only she understood.

Amanda bit her lip and wondered where this was leading. She knew full well there was a double meaning behind his words. His eyes were full of questions she could only guess at and couldn't answer. She blushed, but she didn't answer his question. Instead, she happily accepted Tarik's wife's offer to take her on a tour of the house she'd recently redecorated.

"We've heard so much about you," Tarik's wife said, stopping while Amanda admired the solarium. "I'm so happy you could be with us tonight."

"I was afraid I might be intruding on a family celebration."

"The family is incredibly hospitable," Carolyn said. "Ever since I first met my husband they've been wonderful to me. More wonderful than Tarik at first. I must say, it wasn't love at first sight with us."

"Really? You seem perfectly suited."

"Now, yes. But Tarik was accustomed to giving orders. American women don't take well to taking orders. Especially me. I had my own business and I was used to making decisions on my own. It took him a while, but without giving up a shred of his masculinity, he's the most wonderful, devoted family man." She paused. "But enough about me. Everyone is wondering what went on there at the ski cabin between you and Rahman."

"Nothing, really," Amanda said. The look on Carolyn's face told her she didn't believe her. "I mean of course we got to know each other fairly well. That's only normal after spending all that time together."

"I'm only asking because of how much Rahman's changed," Carolyn said. "He's working hard and has given up his old friends. His parents are very pleased. It was a crowd they didn't approve of, who they considered to be superficial and a bad influence on him. He's suddenly very goal-oriented. We've all wondered exactly what his goal is. He doesn't need money. There's just one thing he doesn't have.'' She paused.

Amanda thought she knew what she was going to say. She didn't want to hear that all he wanted was a woman to share his life. She didn't believe that. He'd told her himself fate had taken away the one love of his life. She changed the subject as adroitly as possible and breathed a sigh of relief when they returned to the living room.

She noticed Rahman talking seriously to his twin brother in the corner. His brother glanced over at Amanda and looked at her while they were talking. She couldn't help wondering if they were talking about her. One by one his family members came up to talk to her, to tell her how much they appreciated what she'd done for Rahman. She couldn't convince anyone she'd only done her job. She assumed that no one knew how she felt about him. She'd told no one. The only one in the world who even guessed her feelings would be Rosie.

They sat down to dinner in the spacious dining room. Glasses were filled with punch and Rahman and his brother made toasts to their parents. They paid homage to their love and devotion that had lasted all these years. For the second time that evening Amanda felt tears in her eyes. The love and affection of this family for each other made her heart swell. This was what she'd missed all these years. Did they know how lucky they were? They couldn't imagine how much she appreciated being included this way, how natural it felt to be toasting the marriage of people she hardly knew, but somehow felt she'd always known them.

The mood lightened as they were served a delicious dinner of roast lamb, tiny new potatoes and creamed spinach. The conversation was lively, filled with family memories as well as plans for the future. Rahman took his share of teasing—about his work schedule, his new attitude, and the change in his life style.

At the end of the table, where Amanda was seated between Rahman and his brother, Rafik asked Amanda what she'd seen of the city. When she confessed she'd not seen much, Rafik leaned over and spoke to Rahman.

"Can't you talk Amanda into staying in the city a little longer, Rahman?" his brother asked. "She hasn't been the Golden Gate Bridge or Alcatraz or Grace Cathedral. She hasn't eaten at Aqua or Chez Panisse."

"Amanda has a mind of her own, Rafik," Rahman said. "There are many things I'd like to talk her into, but she has other patients now and other friends to see the city with. I'm just one of many," he said. The look in his eyes defied her to contradict him. So she did.

"You're not just one of many," she said turning to him and speaking softly. "You're special, Rahman, you know that."

"Then stay," he said, holding her with his level gaze. "Give me a chance…a chance to show you around."

"I thought you were a workaholic these days," she said. "How would you have time."

"I've been working too hard, according to the family," he said quietly while the dinner conversation went on around them. "They'd want me to take a break, especially if it has something to do with you."

"I'll have to call and see if I can get a replacement at the hospital," she said.

He smiled slowly, a dazzling smile that reached his eyes and made his face light up. She refrained from saying, You should do that more often. But the look he gave her told her he knew what she was thinking and that he planned to do a lot more smiling. *If* she stayed around. She felt the warmth of his smile flood her heart. Her whole body trembled with hope and fear. Fear she'd overreacted to this family occasion hope she hadn't misinterpreted his words.

Back at the hotel Rosie promised to find her a replacement for the night shift at the hospital. "I take it this is not totally about sight-seeing," Rosie said.

"No," Amanda said. "I have to see...I have to stay."

"To see if this is really it. If he's the one," Rosie said, sitting on the edge of the bed in the hotel room.

"Yes." It was the first time Amanda had admitted it to Rosie or to herself. She ran her hand over the surface of the desk, back and forth. "I can't go on wondering, imagining..."

"If he loves you as much as you love him," Rosie said.

Amanda gave her a weak smile. "Is it that obvious?"

"Only to me," Rosie said and got up to give her friend a quick hug. "I wish you the best. Because that's what you deserve. And I have a feeling you're going to get it."

For three days Amanda and Rahman played tourist in everybody's favorite city by San Francisco Bay. They rode the cable cars from Market Street over the crest of Nob Hill to Fisherman's Wharf. Rahman sat on the outside bench of the cable car holding Amanda around the waist while she stood and leaned out for the best view, her cheeks pink, her hair flying in the breeze as they rounded the corner.

They rode the ferry across the bay to Tiburon where they ate hamburgers at Sam's Anchor Café on the water and tossed bread crumbs to the gulls. They admired the

view of the sailboats from Coit Tower on Telegraph Hill
while Amanda shivered in the wind off the bay. Rahman
pulled her close to him. She buried her face against his
chest and inhaled the clean smell of his soft wool
sweater, felt the safety and security of his arms around
her and never wanted to leave.

But they did leave. They got back in his car because
they had more places to go and things to see. Rahman
seemed anxious that she see it all, as if she might never
be back. She wondered if he considered this his duty to
show her around. Was that it? Was that why he was
doing this? To discharge his nonexistent obligation to
her?

On the last day he took her to see Grace Cathedral,
the landmark church on top of Nob Hill.

"This is where Carolyn and Tarik were married," he
said as they stood on the steps admiring the Ghiberti
Doors of Paradise. "I want to show you the labyrinth.
That's what impressed me the most. What I've come
back since then to investigate. You see the gray terrazzo
stones that mark the winding path to the center? I don't
know anything about the symbolism of the labyrinth, but
for me the center represents the truth. The truth had always seemed so elusive to me, so hard to define. The
one thing I believed to be constant in this world. Then
one day I stopped by the church and I saw it there, so
clearly, so accessible. I just had to take the right path.
For so long I'd been on the wrong path. Well, you know
about that," he said ruefully.

"The radial joints mark the four points of the com-
pass. And next to it is the meditation garden, which is
my favorite place to think things over. Since I came back
to town I've found coming here has helped me see things

clearer. See the buds on the plum trees? Soon it will be spring and they'll be in bloom."

Amanda didn't say anything. She was so moved by the sight of this place that meant so much to him. It was easy to imagine the garden in bloom, the white blossoms filling the air with a faint perfume. She wondered if she'd see it that way. Or if she'd ever be back. The city would never be the same without him. She'd prefer to keep the memory of these three precious days intact and not spoil them by returning and seeing it by herself or with anyone else.

That night he chose a small neighborhood French restaurant for their last dinner together. Amanda tried to enjoy the entrecote she'd chosen, but her mind wandered. She didn't know how many more times she could say goodbye to Rahman without breaking down completely. It had taken her weeks to get over their last goodbye. She could honestly say she hadn't gotten over it yet. This time she vowed there would be no kisses. She hoped she could control herself better.

Rahman seemed distracted, too. Over coffee he reached for her hand across the table. "Amanda," he said. "Tomorrow you'll be leaving."

Her heart hammered. This was it. This was where he was going to say goodbye. He was just as wary of a scene as she was. So he'd chosen the restaurant where there could be no hugs and no kisses and hopefully no tears either.

"These last few days have been wonderful," she said. "I can't thank you enough."

"Yes, you can," he said, his hand holding hers so tightly she could feel the strength in his touch and feel his pulse beating rapidly. His eyes reflected the light from the candle on the table. "You can thank me by telling me that you love me as much as I love you, that you don't want to leave me, that you'll marry me and…''

"Wait," she said, tears of joy filling her eyes. "I thought…you said…"

"I said a lot of things," he said. "But that was before I got to know you, before I fell in love with you. Before I saw you in the middle of the night in your bathrobe and in the morning before you had your coffee with your hair tousled and I finally realized that my life would be empty without you. That I didn't want to go through life alone. That only you could fill the place in my heart. That I'd been waiting for you my whole life." He paused and looked alarmed at the tears in her eyes. "What is it? Have I said the wrong thing? If you don't feel the way I do, say so before I make a fool of myself even more than I have."

She shook her head wordlessly. She swallowed hard over the lump in her throat.

"You don't have to say anything," he said, mistaking her distress. "I know what you want. You made it perfectly clear to me. You want a family man who knows what he wants and how to get it. You want a small house with a picket fence."

Amanda finally found her voice. "I know what I said. But that was before I met you, Rahman. Before I fell in love with you. Before I saw you recover with courage and strength from a terrible accident. Before I saw you pick up the pieces of your life and go forward. Before you kissed me and made me feel like the most desirable woman in the world. I don't want anything or anybody but you. I can get along without that picket fence but I can't get along without you."

He stared at her, unable to believe the words he'd just

heard. She couldn't get along without him. She loved him.

"I'll get you the fence," he promised, his voice raw and husky with emotion. "I'll get you anything you want. But first, just as a token, I want you to have this ring." He took a small black velvet box from his pocket and gave it to her.

Again her eyes filled with tears as he slipped the diamond ring on her finger. This time he wasn't alarmed. He was the happiest man in the world.

* * * * *

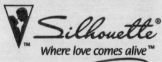

**Where royalty and romance
go hand in hand...**

The series continues in Silhouette Romance
with these unforgettable novels:

HER ROYAL HUSBAND
by Cara Colter
on sale July 2002 (SR #1600)

THE PRINCESS HAS AMNESIA!
by Patricia Thayer
on sale August 2002 (SR #1606)

SEARCHING FOR HER PRINCE
by Karen Rose Smith
on sale September 2002 (SR #1612)

And look for more Crown and Glory stories in
SILHOUETTE DESIRE starting in October 2002!

Available at your favorite retail outlet.

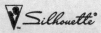

SPECIAL EDITION™

Was it something in the water...
or something in the air?

Because bachelors in Bridgewater, Texas,
are becoming a vanishing breed—fast!

Don't miss these three exciting stories of Texas cowboys by favorite author Jodi O'Donnell:

Deke Larrabie returns to discover
someone *else* he left behind....

THE COME-BACK COWBOY
(Special Edition #1494)
September 2002

Connor Brody meets his match and gives her

THE RANCHER'S PROMISE
(Silhouette Romance #1619)
October 2002

Griff Corbin learns about true
friendship and love when he falls for

HIS BEST FRIEND'S BRIDE
(Silhouette Romance #1625)
November 2002

Available at your favorite retail outlet.

Where love comes alive™

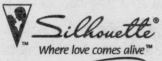

buy books

Your one-stop shop for great reads at great prices. We have all your favorite Harlequin, Silhouette, MIRA and Steeple Hill books, as well as a host of other bestsellers in Other Romances. Discover a wide array of new releases, bargains and hard-to-find books today!

learn to write

Become the writer you always knew you could be: get tips and tools on how to craft the perfect romance novel and have your work critiqued by professional experts in romance fiction. Follow your dream now!

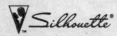

Silhouette®

Where love comes alive™—online...

Visit us at
www.eHarlequin.com

SILHOUETTE *Romance*

COMING NEXT MONTH

#1612 SEARCHING FOR HER PRINCE—Karen Rose Smith
Crown and Glory
Sent to Chicago to find a missing prince, Lady Amira Sierra Corbin
found—and fell for—a gorgeous tycoon. Skeptical of Amira's
motives, Marcus Cordello hid his true identity. Would love conquer
deceit when Amira finally learned the truth?

#1613 THE RAVEN'S ASSIGNMENT—Kasey Michaels
The Coltons: Comanche Blood
Was the presidential candidate leaking secrets that could threaten
national security? Agent Jesse Colton intended to find out—even if it
meant posing as campaign staffer Samantha Cosgrove's boyfriend!
But would this unlikely duo find the culprit…and discover love?

#1614 CAUGHT BY SURPRISE—Sandra Paul
A Tale of the Sea
Beth Livingston's father was convinced that mer creatures existed—
and now had living proof! But was the handsome merman Saegar
willing to become human in order to protect his underwater kingdom
and escape captivity? And what would become of Beth—his new
wife?

#1615 9 OUT OF 10 WOMEN CAN'T BE WRONG—Cara Colter
When Ty Jordan's sister entered him in a contest, 90 percent
of the women declared Ty the most irresistible man in the world!
Ty, however, wasn't interested in their dreams. Could photographer
Harriet Snow convince Ty to make her the object of *his* fantasies?

#1616 MARRIED TO A MARINE—Cathie Linz
Men of Honor
Justice Wilder had led a charmed life—until an injury forced
him to rely on his ex-wife's younger sister. As a physical therapist,
Kelly Hart knew she could help heal his body, but could she
convince Justice that she wasn't another heartless Hart?

#1617 LIFE WITH RILEY—Laurey Bright
Handsome, successful Benedict Falkner wanted the perfect society
wife—*not* someone like Riley Morrissette, his beautiful, free-spirited
housekeeper. Still, the thought of having Riley in his life—in his
bed!—was nearly irresistible.…